To

MW01144507

With very best wishes

Louise Gherasim

GRAINNE

Sailor Princess of Ireland

Louise Gherasim

MINERVA PRESS

LONDON
ATLANTA MONTREUX SYDNEY

First Published 1998 by
MINERVA PRESS
195 Knightsbridge
London SW7 1RE

Printed in Great Britain for Minerva Press

GRAINNE
Sailor Princess of Ireland

To my beloved husband, Teodor,
who has been a continual support and encouragement.

Foreword

Grainne, pronounced Graw-nya, was a real Irish princess who lived in the sixteenth century in the west of Ireland. She became a very strong woman. She ruled her people with kindness and consideration. She was captain of her own ships trading with France and Spain. She was one of the few Gaelic rulers able to hold on to her lands and possessions in a time when England tried to take over all of Ireland.

Today, young girls can still learn from Grainne. Her courage, her determination, and especially her love of learning led her to achieve great things against all odds, in a world where even brave men failed.

Louise Gherasim
July 23, 1997
Tigard, Oregon

Acknowledgments

I wish to thank my very dear friend, Jane Bly for her careful and patient typing of the manuscript and Damian Russell for his painstakingly accurate editing. Without these two wonderful people this little book would not have materialized.

Chapter One

The small girl stood on the headland. The outcropping of jagged black rocks contrasted starkly with the bright saffron of her long woolen skirt and ivory bodice. Grainne didn't like girl's clothes. She usually wore trews. But when she was forced by her mother to wear a skirt, as she was on this special occasion, she always hitched it up like a baggy breeches. This gave her freedom to run and jump and ride her pony.

For the past month, she had been carefully wiping off the days on her slate calendar. Now that she had cleaned off the last day, she had raced to the headland and stationed herself in her present position.

Hour after hour, she waited. Searching the mists with anxious dark eyes, she sought to penetrate the grayness for sight of her father's vessels.

Her heart rose and sank with the billowing waves as an emerging blob became no more than a fisherman's curragh returning with the day's catch.

She could not tell the color of the sky. Only the color of the sea, she knew. Gray and black and blacker hills of white-topped water. Not even the islands, those closest to her father's land, were visible. For the fog was thick and covered the whole world, even reaching across the bay to her home, the stone fortress of Belclare.

Yes, Grainne Ui Maille, Grace O'Malley in the English tongue, was, at eight years old, very familiar with the colors of the sea. She knew them in all their various hues. She knew the happy tints and the bad-tempered shades. For Grainne, like her seafaring father, was a child of the sea.

Hoarse throated gulls circled overhead but no other sound broke through the constant pounding sound of the breakers.

She was born hearing the song of the waves, had spent her early childhood playing in the crystal eddies, and had ridden the rolling breakers in the bay many times in her father's ships.

Father! The word brought warm feelings to little Grainne. She worshipped her father, Owen 'Dubhdarra' (Black Oak) O'Malley, who was chieftain of the Barony of Murrisk, a large stretch of land on Ireland's western seacoast.

Suddenly, her heart missed a beat. She was afraid. It was growing late. She felt the chill in the air that told her that the late autumn sun was low on the horizon behind the fog.

What if her father did not return? She had heard of the fighting that sometimes took place out on the sea. No sooner had the thought occurred to her than she knew what she had to do.

Leaving her lookout on the promontory, she ran, past the stone fortress to the Murrisk Abbey looming large and forbidding through the fog, and right to the church. The huge wooden doors were open. But it was very dark within. Only the beeswax candles burned in the sanctuary giving a faint flickering light. The main altar was scarcely visible.

Grainne knew that God lived in the little house with the golden door which occupied the center of the altar. She knew because the good Father Abbot had told her. And her soft-spoken mother, who attended the services regularly, also reminded her to be on her best behavior when in God's Presence.

She also knew that her grandparents for several generations were buried in this church, for she had read their names on the stone walls. In fact, the abbey had been built by her family in 1457 for the Augustinian Friars. But this evening she did not have time to think of these things; she had more immediate concerns. She had to remind God that her father was on his way home. Perhaps he needed God's help at that very moment. If God could do everything, as Father Abbot had said, then He surely could bring her father back safely that very night.

A soft rain had begun to fall when Grainne emerged from the dark interior of the church. It was growing dusk but she was not afraid and immediately ran back again to her lookout. She seated herself on a large flat rock. The grumbling sounds in her stomach told her it was long past supper time. She had risen before everyone else in the large household and had run off without her breakfast. How could she eat? She was too excited. It had been such a long time since she had seen her beloved father. Now she wanted to be the first to see his galleys as they sailed gracefully between the islands. In her mind's eye she could imagine their huge sails full and white above the ash-gray scudding clouds on the horizon. This was the day, she felt sure, that she so long awaited: the day her father would come home from the sea.

Her father, Lord of Upper Umhall, was king of the seas. It said as much on the Blue Ensign at the mast-head of the *Santa Cruz*, her father's ship: *Terra Marique Potens* – Powerful by Land and Sea. She knew the words in four languages.

Grainne also knew that every ship, big or small, that sailed the waters off the north-western coast had to pay tribute to her father. He was indeed a great chieftain and all his people loved him.

She sprang up.

'I, too, will be king of the seas,' she said. Then, in a loud voice that scattered the gulls and the smaller terns near the waterline, 'I will be king, I will be king of the seas and all the lands around them!'

The gulls, those forever hungry scavengers, had withdrawn to further, more plenteous feeding grounds as the tide receded. Grainne's heart sank as she realized that, as each rippling wave left traces of its kelp-strewn tracks farther and farther out on the sandy shore, it would be too late for her father's ships to make land. Even the shelter of the cove on the leeward side of the promontory was too shallow. She may as well go back to the Castle and get something to eat. It would be early morning now before the next tide.

'Oh, father,' she sighed as she got up wearily from the damp rock. Then gathering her heavy skirt above her ankles, she ran home to the warmth of the turf fire and a steaming bowl of oatmeal porridge.

Chapter Two

'And where do you think you're off to now?' asked
Bridget, a serving woman. 'Your Lady mother would
have you attend her straight away.'

Grainne was stopped before she could reach the
door leading to the *bawn*.[1]

'I wish to attend my Father,' she flung back defiantly in a low, hoarse voice. The order to wait on her
mother was completely ignored.

She pulled away from the servant and ran out to the
inner yard and the early morning calling to her hound,
Cu, as she went.

Grainne would accept her mother's scolding later.
Her only thought now was to reach the docking area
before it was too late.

Grainne climbed on top of a stone wall, the better
to see in all directions. A clear patch was visible out to
sea. The mists and fogs of early morning had begun to
fade as a watery sun broke through. But still there was
no sign of any ships out on the gray horizon.

She jumped down. The ground beneath her feet
was rutted. It bore the imprints of many horses' hoofs
and the long winding curves of carts and carriages.
Grainne liked to ride in a carriage when it meant a visit

---

[1]   *Bawn* – enclosed yard.

to her grandmother O'Malley, but she absolutely hated having to get all dressed up in her fine velvet gown, and having to sit quietly for such a long journey. But, even that she could put up with, when she thought of the time she would have later. At her grandmother's, she was allowed to wear her oldest clothes and she could get soiled all she liked. She was so happy because she was free. Free of lessons, free of household chores, but, best of all, she was free of her mother's watchful eye and the tiresome rules she made up for her to follow.

Then it happened! As if by magic! The whole bay was full of ships.

Wild with excitement, Grainne raced to the edge of the water. 'Father, Father!' she shouted at the top of her voice. There he was, at last. Her beloved father. How handsome he looked, his black hair falling to his shoulders. His face was covered with a black, neatly trimmed beard. He's always got a goodly look, she told herself.

As soon as he stepped ashore, she was swept up into his arms. 'And what has my sailor princess been doing all this time?' he asked, and his deep voice reminded her of the *bodhran*[2] so often heard in the Castle when he was home.

'Oh, Father, I've so much to tell you.'

As she rode high in her father's arms, she noticed beads of sweat and sea water glistening on his *glib* and beard. His saffron *leine*[3] was soiled. There was even a

---

[2]   *Bodhran* – small drum similar to a tambourine.
[3]   *Leine* – shirt made of linen, also a long gown worn by women.

tear in one of the wide sleeves where it fell through the shorter sleeve of his leather jerkin.

Maybe that's why Father doesn't mind when I get dirty. He's kind of dirty himself, she thought. And then her mind had happy pictures of all the fun and merrymaking there would be now that her father had returned: music, singing, dancing, and best of all, storytelling before the great fire in the long evenings. She snuggled into the soft place beneath his beard.

'There we are,' said Owen as he placed her on the first steps of polished stone that led to the upper floors of the Castle. 'You're all grown up!' He looked at her dark eyes and sallow complexion, so different from her fair mother. She was his child and no doubt about it.

'Bring them along,' said Owen, turning to a servant who had been following with packages in his arms.

The three of them proceeded up to the living quarters on the third floor. Taking the packages from the servant, Owen dismissed him. Handing one large parcel to Grainne, Owen gently enfolded his waiting wife in his strong arms.

Grainne knew there would be kissing and hugging and even a few tears which her mother would gently wipe away with a lace fringed handkerchief. She didn't want to be part of all that.

'*Dar Dia*! 'Tis sure a sorry thing to be a woman,' she mumbled to herself.

However, she soon forgot everything else in her excitement to open the parcel her father had just placed in her hands. What could it be? She tore at the wrappings and when they failed to come undone with the first attempt, she seated herself on the flagstone floor. With both hands free, Grainne was able to attack the bindings more successfully. Inside the thick covering she found a wooden box. Releasing the clasp, she readily opened the lid.

'Aw!' she gasped. For a moment, she was speechless. Then, as the realization of what it was that her beloved father had brought dawned on her, she cried out, 'A ship! My ship! My very own ship. Oh, Father, how did you know?'

'Sometimes fathers know these things,' Owen said, pleased that he had made the right decision. 'It's a model of the Caravel that I just brought back from far-off Spain, *a grá*.'[4] Then Owen turned to his wife. 'I can now haul a far bigger cargo to market, my dear, as I will have only sixty men for a crew.' There was new excitement in his voice. 'Think of it, the sails take the place of the hundred and eighty oarsmen needed in the galleys. I can now haul cargo in place of food for the oarsmen.' He stood with his back to the fire, his hands behind him, his legs apart, the way he often stood on his ship.

Grainne had listened. Everything her father said or did was important to her.

'But, Father, who will do the fighting?' Her anxious eyes betraying her concern.

'Don't worry, alanah[5], the galleys will still be used except for the long trips to Spain and the Continent. The routes I will take and the Caravel's speed is such that I will not require fighting men.'

---

[4] *A grá* – love
[5] *Alanah* – baby.

'Father, can I go with you on your next trip to Spain?' she asked and her eager brown eyes had an excited look.

'That trip is almost a year away,' he replied. 'We will see when the time comes.' He smiled the special smile he had just for her.

'Grainne! Have you lost your wits completely? How could a little girl go on such a journey?' her mother asked.

Grainne looked puzzled. She could never understand her mother.

'Why not? Father will be there,' came the self-confident, self-assured answer. 'And father is the best captain in the world.'

'Hah,' Owen laughed his big deep laugh. 'That's what I like – a lass who knows her own mind and considers naught impossible.'

'Then I can go, Father?' Grainne's intelligent brown eyes grew wider in anticipation.

Owen studied his daughter a moment. Already, she had a way with her. A mere chit of a girl, yet she was able to persuade him to do and say things that even his wife was unable to make him do. What was it about this child that so captivated his heart? That compelled him to grant her every wish? She had a talent. A great talent. He did not know what it was at that exact moment. But he felt that all great women who influenced or ruled others had this gift... Grainne, his Grainne, certainly knew how to handle people. She had persuaded him, almost without his knowing it, to do the very thing he had decided against.

'Father, you're dreaming again!' Grainne said, and tugged at his sleeve.

'As I said, my love, it's a long way off. We will see when the time comes. Fair enough?' For a moment she was silent just standing there looking up into his eyes, searching. A little old woman in a child's body, he thought.

'Now let's talk about tomorrow.' He sat down in his favorite high-backed chair and took her on his knees.

'I have to make a trip across the bay to the Moher O'Malley branch of the clan,' he said, and he turned to his wife, Margaret.

'Since I'll be going close to your parents, Margaret, I'd like to take you both along. 'Twon't take me but a few days to sell the goods. An' in the meantime you'll have a chance to visit your parents...' He again addressed Grainne, 'An' you, your grandparents.'

'Oh, Father, so many nice things happen when you are home,' Grainne said, wild with excitement. She jumped off his lap and danced about clapping her hands. Then she sat on a cushion at his feet.

'Owen, how nice. It's been almost a year since I've seen the family,' said Margaret and she smiled the happy smile she only used for him.

'Well, then it's settled. I thought it would be a good opportunity for you and my little sailor,' Owen O'Malley leaned forward and rumpled the tousled head of his adoring daughter seated at his feet. 'Since I'll be having several days' work, you'll no doubt, have plenty o' time to make trouble.' He laughed.

'That'll be fine, Owen, dear.' Margaret wasn't happy that he encouraged the pranks and unladylike behavior of his only daughter. But, at that moment, she did not want to offend him by speaking her mind.

'Lady Luck was with me, I made some good bargains this trip,' the Lord of Umhall continued. 'And Spain will buy all the *falangai*[6] I can get. I must find more wool, it's a rare chance.'

'We'll get more, Father.' Grainne wanted to encourage him.

Margaret yawned. Such matters never did interest her. 'Now that we're to take a long journey tomorrow, it's time for bed,' she said, turning to Grainne. 'No morning escapades. No flying hither an' yon. I want you here where I can keep an eye on you. I'll not travel with a ragamuffin.' Her mother looked up from her sewing and her pretty blue eyes were cross.

'Oh, no. I didn't have time to talk to father. An' I have so much to...'

'You didn't hear a word I said, Grainne.' Margaret turned in despair to Owen. 'Really, Owen, the child is incorrigible. I can't think what will become of her. She needs a firm hand an' all you do is...'

Owen interrupted, 'Spoil her! That's what your pretty mother thinks, isn't it, lass?' He bent again and lifted his beloved daughter on his knee. 'So you haven't had time to talk to me, eh?'

'Your father is tired, Grainne, and it's long past your bedtime,' observed Margaret, knowing she was fighting a losing battle.

---

[6] *Falanga* – frieze cloak

'Arrah! Sure I'm never too tired to talk to my little sailor,' said her husband. Again Owen ran his fingers through the thickness of Grainne's tangled hair. 'Come, *mo stóirín*,[7] let's away to your bed. We'll be talking while you get your nightshift on. An' I'll tuck you in all cozy an' warm.'

Grainne stood up and looked at her father a moment. The great love of her small heart was burning in her dark eyes. 'You're the best father in the whole world.' Then she threw her arms around his neck, and, as he gathered her up in a warm hug, even her beautiful new gift was completely forgotten in the supreme joy of the moment.

---

[7] *Mo stóirín* – my treasure

Chapter Three

Owen joined his wife once more at the fireplace. His favorite wolfhound, Boru, lifted his head, wagged a lazy tail, and then, as soon as his master was seated, settled down to sleep again.

'She's sound asleep. All tuckered out she was, the wee thing.' He looked at Margaret as he spoke but she merely smiled. Owen stretched his legs. He was tired himself but he wanted to enjoy the warmth of the turf fire and the comfort of his home on this his first night. As he watched the purple dancing flames, he remembered the morning some eight years before when his baby daughter was born.

''Tis a girl! 'Tis a girl!' the servants shouted from one to the other around the Castle at Belclare.

It was the second of July, the year of Our Lord 1530, when a tiny, red-faced, black-haired little creature, with a pair of lungs that left no doubt in the minds of all about her health, saw the light of day.

'Sir, you're the father of the largest, squirmiest, loudest, baby girl I've ever brought into this world,' shouted Una Murphy as she prepared the baby for its blanket.

Owen had been married to Margaret for over five years. They had almost given up hope of ever having a baby. 'Then God had been good to them and sent them a little girl,' Margaret said proudly.

On the ninth day after her birth, the baby was baptized in the Abbey of Murrisk and named Grainne. Her father said no other name was necessary as she was a very special Grace from heaven.

As soon as the little one could toddle, she was looked upon as an extraordinary child. She was intelligent and mature beyond her years and curious about everything.

When she was five, she started school in the nearby convent. Soon, she took lessons in Latin, Spanish, and geography from the monks at the Abbey. This was not because she was a chieftain's daughter but because of her quick mind and eagerness to learn. She was the only girl attending the Abbey school at the time.

But Owen wanted his daughter to know other things as well. So every spring and summer he would take her along with him as he went to check over his lands and the people living on them. At first, she didn't understand what was going on in the noisy world surrounding the Castle. But by the time she was eight, only her father knew more.

All around the Castle were scattered the thatched cottages, huts, and stone cabins of the servants, workmen, and other followers of the O'Malley clan. There were also fifteen or twenty buildings that served as storage sheds, smoke-houses, barns, and work places for the clan's trading ships.

As Owen took little Grainne's hand, he would patiently explain everything to her.

'This is the shed where the hides are cured and stored. See that pretty skin. That's a deer,' he said.

'I know that one!' the small voice piped up. 'It's a squirrel.'

'You're perfectly right. An' that's an otter. Over there, you see? There are some fine fox furs.'

'An' what is that for?' she asked, pointing to a frame.

'A good question. That is called a frame an' on it the skins are stretched and dried.'

They walked on. Owen inspecting the quality of the hides. His little daughter listening to his comments and learning all she could.

'These will be used to make a soft leather which can then be made into fine ladies' gloves, slippers, and gentlemen's jerkins.'

'I know what the pretty furs will be used for, Father,' began Grainne.

Owen smiled. He guessed that his clever wee daughter had a special motive for directing his attention to the furs.

'Then tell me what you think,' he replied.

'This one will be a winter cloak for mama,' said Grainne, hesitating; she carefully checked the entire furs that were on display. First, she looked over the colors; then, she checked to see that the pelt was flawless, perfectly intact. She didn't want something that was torn. 'Mmm... this one,' she murmured. She had chosen an excellent skin. 'This one, Father, will make such a pretty winter *bratt*[1] for me.'

---

[1]   *Bratt* – cloak; spelled with two t's for English readers.

'Hah, hah, hah, I declare, you'll ruin your father, yet. Do you know you've chosen the most expensive fur in the entire stock?'

'Oh, Father, you've got lots of others an' I do like this one best.'

'But you have a fine winter bratt already, a grá.'

'It's getting small. It's up to here.' Grainne said, pointing to her shin.

'Then 'tis growin' fast you are. Aye, indeed, too fast. Well, I suppose we can't have you getting cold this winter, can we now?'

Grainne beamed at her smiling father. 'Sure I knew you'd let me have it.'

'Shhh... it's our secret now,' answered Owen, putting his index finger to his lips.

'All right, Father, I won't tell a one.'

Owen continued to examine the furs.

'Father, what will you do with the rest of these?' asked his daughter.

'The best will go to the cold countries of Europe, mostly to the Netherlands, Germany, and northern Italy where they will be made into hoods, muffs, and cloaks, and some will even be fashioned into high winter boots.'

'With the furry part turned inside? Mm... that would be so comfy and warm! Can I have fur boots, Father?'

'Our winters don't get that cold. I think your wool stockings keep you warm enough, don't they?'

Grainne thought a moment. 'I s'ppose... but it would be nice to have a pair of fur boots,' she replied.

By the time they had reached the smoke-house, Grainne had persuaded her father that the fur boots would be a good present for her next birthday.

The pungent smell of burning turf and oak wood permeated the air around the closed huts.

'I like that smell, Father.'

'Then you know all about the smoke huts, eh?'

''Course, Father,' said Grainne with a sort of superior air. 'I can tell you all the different kinds of fish that you've got in there.' She looked to see if her father was really paying attention.

'I listened to Duggan when he was preparing the fish an' then I said the names over and over again till I knew them by heart. Want to hear? I made them rhyme.'

'I'm listening, lass.' Owen was looking around for one of the men who usually worked in the smoke huts. 'Ah, there you are, Duggan. Havin' trouble finding enough of the right kind of wood?'

Duggan and his companion, Fergus, had just arrived on the scene leading a donkey laden with wood.

'No sir, not yet anyway. Have to go much farther than last year, but I think we can manage fine enough,' answered Duggan.

'Father,' said Grainne, tugging at her father's sleeve. 'I'm waiting.'

'Yes, a grá.' Owen had completely forgotten about what his small daughter wanted so badly to tell him. 'What does my Sailor Princess want?'

'Oh, Father! You forgot. My fish poem!' Grainne wrinkled her face, she was impatient with her father sometimes. How could he forget?

'Ah, sure enough. 'Tis distracted I am, at times. Now tell me your poem, a grá.'

'Duggan an' Fergus you can listen too.' She puffed out her chest as she addressed the workmen.

Owen gave the men a quick wink. Pulling an exaggerated pose of attentiveness, the two men ceased unloading the donkey and gave their attention to the small girl.

'We're all waiting.'

'Yes, Father.' She moistened her lips and opening her pretty mouth, took a big breath, and recited.

> 'There's salmon and hake,
> Mackerel and trout,
> Cod fish and herring,
> Flatfish, no doubt!
> There's haddock, there's eel,
> There's oysters and crab,
> Cockles and mussels
> An' shrimp that smells bad.'

Grainne was swept up into the strong arms of her happy father.

''Tis the proud man I am to have such a clever daughter!' he said as the men applauded. Then, kissing her, he set her on her feet again.

'Aye, indeed. A right clever lass is our Grainne,' said Duggan. 'Be takin' your place in no time at all, sir, that she will.'

'Yes, Duggan. I'm sure you're right,' said Owen, and again winked at the men. 'I'll be spending my old age in peace and quiet. My Grainne will be able to take over everything.'

Grainne was so happy to have pleased her father especially in front of the serving men, that she excused him for having kissed her in public. That kind of thing was fine for her mother but she didn't want to be treated like a little girl. She just didn't want to have anything to do with girl things.

Father and daughter continued on their rounds hand-in-hand. The next building contained many wooden vats of meat; pork and beef, mostly, but there were some barrels put aside for the salting of fish also.

A large building and one set apart from the others by a small flower garden was now within sight. Its thatch had been lately renewed. It looked very clean and attractive with its window boxes of bright red geraniums which contrasted with the fresh white-washed exterior. Inside, a great open fire at one end kept the room comfortable.

'Mornin' Bridie,' said Owen. 'An' how's the work?'

'Fine, fine entirely, sir.'

Bridie was in charge of the six to ten women who were busy from early morning till late into the night with the looms. It was in this beehive of activity that Grainne would learn the art of making clothes; weaving, dyeing, designing, and sewing.

Yes, Owen thought, his little girl was growing up too fast. He was troubled. Soon, she would be a woman. But she so wanted to go to Spain with him. Perhaps Margaret was right. He had doubts. Maybe it wasn't fitting for a young lady to travel day after day with rough sailors. There wasn't much privacy on board his ship either. Oh well, he didn't have to decide tonight; it was still a long way off. He would, as he told Grainne, decide when the time came.

When Owen and Grainne returned late in the evening, Margaret was waiting. Always beautifully dressed, she wore a long *leine*. Over this gown, she wore a sleeveless blue dress of fine linen. Her thick golden braids were kept in place with a roll of linen head cloth. And, as always, she was smiling, happy to greet her husband.

The perfume of lavender water floated around her. Her skin was flawless and when she smiled, as she often did when Owen was at home, she was very beautiful.

In Grainne's eyes her mother represented everything that was feminine and soft. It seemed that her only object in life was to please her husband. She had no ambitions for herself. This Grainne, even at so young an age, did not understand.

As a consequence, mother and daughter never saw eye to eye. Margaret had failed to pass on the most rudimentary feminine skills to her outspoken, loud, and self-opinionated daughter. Even the sisters in the convent school had given up the idea of teaching her the art of stitchery. In Sister Enda's words, 'The baby chicks in the hen runs could manage to make straighter strokes than Grainne can on her sampler.'

But Grainne didn't care. She was always proud when she was told that she resembled her father rather than her mother. And she was happy that she was growing up as her father's 'son' and not her mother's daughter.

When Owen had tucked his Sailor Princess into bed, he joined his wife. He took his place beside the fire and watched her as she plied the embroidery needle so nimbly. As he looked at her beautiful face, he realized that it had been thirteen years since first he had brought her to his home here in Belclare. Time had slipped away. But, she was still lovely.

'You're still the most beautiful woman in all of Connaught, *Margaret Ni Conchobhar Óg Mac Conchobhair mic Maoilseachloinn.*'

'Ah, go on with you, Owen O'Malley.'

She raised her golden head. And when Owen looked into her shining clear blue eyes, he knew he was in love all over again.

Margaret was tall and slim. She walked with such grace that at times she seemed to float, to glide from one place to another.

Owen was very proud of her. He left the hearth and drew close to his wife. On one knee, he gently took her hand. For a moment, he contemplated its beauty. Then remembering his younger days, he lightly kissed each delicate fingertip.

'You're truly a queen.' The pride and love were evident in his dark eyes. 'Come, my Queen, let's away to our bed. All too soon a new day begins.'

Chapter Four

'Mmmmm... Sure smells good,' said Grainne as she stepped into the dining-hall. The table was prepared for the morning meal.

'You'll be wanting your porridge, I suppose,' said Bridget as Grainne skipped across the flagstone floor towards the open hearth where the maidservant was busy stirring a large pot of oatmeal gruel.

'With lots of honey and cream.'

'Now, now, you know what your Lady mother says. "One spoon o' honey and milk, no cream."'

'*Dar Dia*! Mama won't know if you don't tell her. Anyway, Father says honey's good for me,' Grainne said defiantly.

'Grainne, you're a naughty girl. You know what happens to children who don't obey their parents?'

''Spose you're going to tell me the *púca*[1] will take me away.' She pursed her mouth challenging the servant.

'Ah, I'm thinking since you know so much you might be afraid,' answered Bridget.

'Hah, an' why would I be afraid if I don't believe?'

The servant threw up her arms in horror and her mouth opened wide.

---

[1]   *Púca* – evil spirit.

'Shee... is it denying the wee folk ye are? Mayhap you'll be telling me that I didn't, myself, hear the banshee[2] not three nights since.' Bridget crossed herself and shook her head. The child is surely 'touched' to say such things, she thought, but she had no time to argue with her this morning. Before long the Lord and Lady of the Castle would be awaiting their breakfast.

Grainne was served. The servant had no more time to pay attention to her. She was free! Free to help herself to another spoon of honey and to float her porridge on a thick sea of cream.

Before Grainne had finished, she heard the booming bass voice of her father as he greeted the individual members of his household.

'Mornin', Seamus,' Owen called to his *rechtaire*, the man who took his place around the Castle when he was away. 'We'll be for Moher O'Malley country this morning.'

'Right you are, sir,' answered Seamus.

'We'll take the galley *Faoilan*. You can be telling the men. I'll be along presently.'

'Can I go to watch, Father? Can I, can I?' Grainne bounded to the low wooden trestle table where her father had already seated himself.

'You here so early? Now what did your mother say last night?'

'Oh, no, Father, no. I don't want to stay here till the ship's ready. Mama will make me sit for hours and hours.' The sunny smile had left her face.

---

[2] *Banshee* – fairy woman – associated with death.

Owen looked at his daughter's troubled features. He couldn't bear to see the happiness leave those great brown eyes.

'What am I to do with you, at all? Your mother will have my hide if you dare leave this house this morning.'

'No, she won't. Not this time, Father. She's so happy you're home, she'll pretend to be angry.' Grainne was so confident, that her father chuckled in spite of himself.

As she coaxed, Owen grew weaker. His heart melted and he could no longer refuse her. Margaret would be furious. A feeling of guilt also troubled him. The wee girl would suffer later. She it was that would bear the brunt of her mother's fury. He'd have to make excuses for her, for her wilfulness, her misdemeanors, her disobedience, her lack of the finer feminine graces. The list went on and on. 'Ah, a pox on it!' he muttered. He took Grainne between his knees and looked at her full in the face. 'You know what your mother will say.'

Grainne nodded her head.

'An' you're ready to take the consequences?'

'*Dar Dia*! Father, you must be getting soft... like a woman, eh?'

'Hah, Hah, hah!' Owen threw back his head and let the rafters catch the sound of his mighty laugh. Then, as if to ease his conscience, he said, 'Ah, sure you're never going to learn all tied up in silks and satins. You're the only "son" I've got. Get your *bratt*. Let's go, before I change my mind.'

Grainne stood on the prow of the *Faoilan* with her father as he supervised the loading of the great galley. It was a clear morning. A steady wind from the sea with the bite of winter in its jaws kept things churned up. The heavy ropes beat against the mast. The ship swayed on the uneven swells.

'This must be one of the biggest ships in the world!' Grainne looked down at the great ship. Thirty oarsmen were getting ready to take this monster out to sea.

Her father's pride was obvious. 'Well, no, not the biggest. But it's pretty close. Only the great galleons of the Spanish Royal fleet are bigger.'

'Bigger than this? I'd sure like to see them.'

For the next two hours the men worked steadily. There were fine wines from the vineyards of Spain, silk cloth from the looms of Venice, spices from the far off islands that bore that name, and a special gift for Moher O'Malley's wife, a fine tapestry from Denmark.

Grainne stood a little apart watching her father as he gave orders to the men. At such times, Owen cut an imposing figure. He stood tall on the prow, observing all: a man who was no longer young but who still possessed robust vigor and vitality. Grainne studied his features; his handsome face, clean-cut, strong, straight nose, firm chin, head held high. Grainne adored her father, 'Dubhdarra.' He was a strong leader. He demanded respect; he administered justice; he knew how to win the loyalty of his followers. He would bend to no one. This he had proved many times, for he was one of the few Irish Lords left who never acknowledged the English crown.

As she watched, the west wind tossed his dark shoulder-length hair and rumpled the fresh cut glib on his forehead. She knew she wanted more than anything else in the world to be like her father. She took notice of every movement and every word. He showed firmness and decision. He was a man to be obeyed.

She admired his dress. Although she never cared too much for clothes herself, she realized that he had taste. He was so different from the common sailor, with his saffron *leine*, its richly embroidered sleeves falling in wide folds through the shorter sleeves of his black tanned leather jerkin. She noted his highly polished black leather boots.

Owen adjusted the Tara brooch[3] on his cloak. The precious stones in the large gold pin caught the opal shafts of the midday light. As the breeze tugged at the long folds of his heavy woolen mantle, the ivory handled skene at his waist was visible and reminded Grainne that being a sea captain had its danger as well as its romance. And, once again, she longed for the day when she could ply the high seas and accompany him to sunny Spain. She just had to find a way.

Grainne and her father returned to the Castle as soon as the ship was loaded. The anticipated scolding from her mother did not materialize, as she had predicted. Margaret had been too busy packing, giving orders to the servants, and taking care of the household chores to have time to spend running after Grainne.

---

[3] *Tara brooch* – ancient broach worn on the shoulder to keep cloak in place.

By early afternoon, they were on their way. Slowly, the great galley moved over the waters of Clew Bay. Grainne was wild with excitement. She had prevailed upon her mother to allow her to wear her trews, but she had to promise to change before landing.

Owen proudly pointed out to his eager daughter all the lands that, despite all odds, had remained in the O'Malley possession.

'Never forget, a grá, that your heritage belongs to the ages. You are descended from Brian Orbsen, King of Connaught. His death is said to have been in 388. That's going back a mighty long time.'

'That's even before St. Patrick came to Ireland!' Grainne was visibly impressed.

'You know, in the beginning, the O'Malley lands were called *Umhalls* and were made up of the baronies of Murrisk and Burrishoole.

'That must have been almost as big as Ireland!'

'Not quite,' and he smiled at her. 'But a goodly portion none the less, because the barony of Murrisk to the south of Clew Bay included the islands of Clare, Inishturk and all the smaller islands of the Bay as well. The barony of Burrishoole on the north side of the Bay initially included Achill. These two baronies were called *Unhall Ui Mhaille* or the Two Owels.

'With the coming of the Normans in the year 1171, all Ireland underwent change. By the year 1235, the O'Malleys in the far western parts of the country, who, for over a thousand years had ruled their lands in relative peace and prosperity, were also affected.' 'Dubhdarra' fell silent and a furrow creased his broad bronzed forehead.

Grainne knew her father had a worried look. She drew closer and took his hand. Giving it a little squeeze, she hoped to impart some small comfort to the strong man whom she felt needed it at that moment.

He looked down at her and his face immediately brightened.

''Tis you're the crafty one,' he said. 'Trying to read my mind, is it you are?' And he took her upturned chin in his other hand. 'Then, let me tell you, for you'll have to know sooner or later, the times we live in are no better than those I've just told you about.'

'You mean the Normans are coming again?' she asked, and there was a flicker of fear in her anxious eyes.

Still looking straight at her, 'Dubhdarra' could scarcely keep from laughing.

'No, the Normans we have managed to civilize but the *Sasanach*...'

'I heard m'lord the Abbot talk of the *Sasanach*. I've a mind, he's fearful of them,' said Grainne.

'Hah, no doubt, fearful of losing his easy living, I'll wager.'

Grainne raised her eyebrows. Her father didn't often speak so bluntly of the monks in her presence. 'Are you afeared, Father?' she asked.

'Dubhdarra' laughed and threw his head back. 'Afeared? Never! As long as I live, no *Sasanach* will set foot on O'Malley territory.'

And Grainne felt the strength of his words in the hard pressure of his strong hands.

He continued, 'Besides, we O'Malleys are a stubborn lot with a tenacious instinct for survival.'

Grainne was satisfied. Her father would take care of the *Sasanach*. She might even tell that to the Lord Abbot the next time she saw him.

'But how did we win over the Normans, Father?'

'Ah, time and example are good teachers,' he answered. 'Our Norman cousins came to realize the wealth and beauty of the culture that surrounded them. They had, over the years, changed their rough uncultured ways, for they were soldiers, warlords, unlettered men for the most part. They adopted the traditions and the customs of the Gael. They learned the Irish language. They donned the dress and followed the Brehon Laws, and in so many ways had they become one with their Irish relatives that it was said of them, "They have become more Irish than the Irish themselves." Finally, in 1342, De Burgo – our neighbor to the east – renounced his allegiance to the English crown and called himself by the traditional title of an Irish Lord, the Mac William Iochtar, Chief of the Bourkes of Mayo.'

He paused; then his daughter remarked, 'Mayhap the *Sasanach* will learn also.' And she looked up at her father again hoping to see him nod his head.

But 'Dubhdarra' was no longer listening. They were nearing the mouth of the Bay. As he sailed his galley out into the waters of the mighty Atlantic, he found a powerful pride swelling in his broad chest. A man would have to travel far to see the likes of all this. His lands, ranging from the fair and fertile pastures of the far eastern boundary to the wild and inhospitable islands of the western sea.

Grainne sensed the pride in her father's heart. She stepped up to him and again took his hand and she knew he had forgotten the Normans and even the *Sasanach*.

He pressed it tenderly and looked down into her upturned face. The breeze caught and blew her dark hair in all directions. She pushed it from her eyes and tried to tame it with her free hand.

'Were I a boy, I wouldn't have to bother with all of this,' she complained.

Owen laughed. ''Tis you're the strange one. I've never known a woman who was not proud of her hair. And here you are complaining of your one beauty.'

Sailing along the rugged coast, Owen pointed out the innumerable inlets, coves, and narrows. Secretive places, he told Grainne, where skiffs and curraghs and even galleys could easily be hidden in time of peril. A coastline so indented, so broken, so treacherous that only the local seafaring people had any knowledge of its perilous reefs. And, even they, at times, could be deceived, for in winter storms, no other coast in Europe was so savage. In spring and autumn, it was a place of perpetual mists so thick that every vestige of a safe and familiar haven was obscured.

'But in summer, my Grainne, when the seas tumble between shades of emerald and azure blue and the still cold waters boil with marine life, the O'Malley fleets sweep over these waters, a veritable army, and dare any, friend or foe, challenge our right to do so!'

The day was far spent when they reached their destination. Grainne was hastily dressed in her velvet gown which covered her right down to her new leather slippers. Her tangled curls were brushed too quickly for comfort and then tightly tied with a velvet ribbon. She was humiliated opposite the sailors but especially when Brien, the ship's boy, came running by, she wished that the sea would come crashing over her.

'Grainne! No, can't be. You look so... so...'

'Oh, go away. What do you know? Stop gawking.' She took a step toward him ready with closed fists if he dared say another word.

But the restraining hand of her mother prevented what would have surely become a raging battle, and most certainly have had disastrous results for her velvet gown.

Grainne, realizing that it was impossible to break away from her mother's grasp and that Brien had sped on agile legs to the far end of the ship, gave up struggling and stood with bowed head at her mother's side.

''Tis time to go. Are you ready, Margaret?' Her father's voice, rich and deep caused her to raise her head.

'We're ready to row you both ashore. Come, I'll hand you over the side, Grainne.'

Glad to be away from her mother's firm grip, Grainne bounded forward.

'What's up? You don't look too happy,' he said.

'I'll be happy when I can get this thing off,' she answered, pulling at her pretty dress.

Her father laughed, and as he handed her to the waiting curragh, he whispered, 'Never mind, my Sailor

Princess, you'll rule them all one day and then you can wear what you like.'

Grainne's brown eyes filled up with tears as she looked into her father's dark face. He alone knew her thoughts; he only knew the heart of his little girl.

Chapter Five

The whole house was filled with the odors of roasting venison, lamb, and poached salmon. Grainne, who had only a mug of buttermilk upon her arrival at her grandparents', was ravenous. She just couldn't wait for supper.

As in her own home in Belclare, meals were served on low trestle tables. Soon the servants came carrying large wooden plates of steaming hot meats. Accompanying these dishes were bowls of fresh vegetables, cabbage, onions, and wild watercress. All were washed down with the mead for which the area was famous – 'the mead-abounding Murrisk.' But this was a very special occasion, the arrival of 'Dubhdarra' and his family. To honor the guests, some rare wines from Spain and France, which Owen had just delivered, were also served. The meal finished with *dellisk*[1] and butter.

When everyone had eaten well, the visitors were entertained by O'Rourke, the local bard.

As the old man ran his bony fingers across the harp strings, Grainne heard the wind sing in the great stone chimney. It was a friendly wind and would carry the fishermen home safely, she knew. Like her father, she

---

[1]
Dellisk – edible seaweed.

had inherited a unique gift. She could tell the signs in the seas and the sky and knew what the winds were saying.

She found a place on a pillow close to her father's feet. She would have liked to crawl up on his lap, but thought better of it since there were so many strangers in the hall.

The old bard grunted. He withdrew a sliver of bone he had been using to dislodge the fragments of mutton between his crooked stained teeth. He rubbed his aged dry hands together and held them out, palms facing the ruddy embers. A serving girl placed a pile of new turf on end.

Grainne watched in anticipation. She knew the familiar overtures to an evening of storytelling. The smell of the coarse woolen garment that covered the bard's body reached her where she sat looking up into her beloved father's face. She turned to watch the bard again. His thin white beard danced against his wrinkled throat. Again, a rumble deep in his chest signaled his intention to speak. All became silent, attentive.

Like cascading water, the sounds gushed from the harp. And, above the ebb and flow, the bard's voice sang: 'As the howling winds, crying from the five fifths of this glorious land, bring with them good and ill, so also do the songs fashioned by human breath carry tales both fair and foul. Some tell of brave deeds, of noble feats, others lament the passing of saintly kings or the betrayal of a loved one. But, tonight my voice will tell of the ancient sagas of the great and proud house of Ui Maille:

"Twas the year eleven an' sixty-seven.'

He paused and looked at his audience with beady blue eyes. Satisfied that he had everyone's attention, he continued:

> *'When Patrick Ui Maille*
> *Set sail in his galley,*
> *To France, he would go*
> *With his hull sunk down low*
> *His cargo, soft wools, meats, and hides.'*

With the chanting of the story of her ancestors, Grainne grew sleepy. It had been a long day. Despite her best efforts, she lapsed into a dream world. A world where all was warmth, color, and romance. She was one with that world and felt the pride her father knew when he spoke to her earlier of his ancestors.

The bard sounded a minor chord, significant, foreboding. Grainne roused herself. She didn't want to miss anything new.

> *'Then one bright sunny day*
> *From the shores of Clew Bay*
> *He set sail with the tides*
> *And his cargo of hides.*
> *Seven days out to sea*
> *In his sturdy galley*
> *Three pirate ships, he espied.'*

'Aw!' A startled gasp escaped Grainne, but she quickly covered her open mouth with her hand, as her eyes grew large with anxiety.

'Then sounding the cry
Patrick swore he would die
Before losing his crew
When enemy fire he drew.
A great battle was fought
But Patrick lost naught.
With courage he bore
Saber, rapier, and sword.
Till ere the end of that day
His cowardly enemy lay
Vanquished and dead.'

Grainne clapped her hands. But a glare from the old man silenced her; he wasn't finished.

'Then for fair France he sped
And triumphantly led
His crew and galleys
O'er the roughest of seas.
When his cargo he'd sold,
For great profit in gold,
Once more he set forth
For native home port.
Both with consummate skill
And indomitable will,
He returned to the fold
As the heroes of old.'[2]

---

[2] Source unknown.

The bard continued to strum for some moments as if he didn't want to finish his tale. Then, with a flourish and several rippling arpeggios, he concluded. He stood, bowed to his audience, and once more took his seat.

There was an outburst of applause. Grainne heard her father call for a flagon of grog for the old man. When he had well drunk, Grainne knew there would be more storytelling. In order not to be sent off to bed, she rubbed her eyes and tried to look wide awake.

It was growing very late, long past Grainne's bedtime, when O'Rourke decided he had sung his way through as many tales as the household could support for one evening. He pulled his bratt around his shoulders. Then, with a flourish, he arose and nodding ever so slightly out of respect for the honored guests, he limped away from the hearth.

Slowly, reluctantly, the audience came to life. The spell was broken. Owen sat up, called for a *giolla*[3] to replenish the empty wine carafes and mead goblets and applauded the bard loud and long and lustily.

'It's time you were in bed, Grainne.' Her mother's treble voice sounded above the booming bass of 'Dubhdarra.' Grainne was reluctant to leave. The magic of it. The glowing peat fire with the dancing figures from the past. The luxury of her father's presence. Would that this time might never end. She continued to sit holding on to the pictures in the flames, in her mind...'

★

---

[3] *Giolla* – servant.

Grainne didn't remember how she had got to bed the night before. The birds were making a terrible racket outside her window when she awoke. For a moment, she was not sure where she was... then, all at once, it dawned on her and she was out of bed in a flash.

Her father would be setting sail again. Perhaps he had already departed.

She wanted to go with him. It was nice to see her grandparents, but it was much nicer to be with her father. She had so much to learn about the ships and the secret places. She knew that one day she would need the knowledge that only her father could give her. She, it was who would take his place. She and she alone.

She pulled on her trews and scrambled into her bodice. She grabbed her bratt and was halfway down the stairs before she realized that she had forgotten her shoes. Back she ran to fetch them, but didn't wait to put them on.

She raced through the great hall, past the many servants and giollas busy about their morning chores. No one took any notice of her. She arrived at the waterfront a short time later, still carrying her shoes, only to find that the *Faoilan* was no longer moored off the shore.

'Father! Oh, Father, how could you?' She sat down on a pile of stones with a heavy heart. The tears welled up in her dark eyes. She would not cry. Grainne Ni Malley would not cry. She clenched her jaws together tightly and forced the tears to go back from where they had come. She had nobody to blame but herself. She hadn't told her father that she wanted to go with him.

Slowly, she put on her shoes. She wouldn't, couldn't go back to the house just yet.

She decided to take a walk along the shore. It was a nice day and the sea winds seemed to call to her.

After a short time, she could go no further. She had simply run out of land. So she climbed the cliff facing her, thinking to return by the higher ground.

Upon reaching the top, she had a fine view. In front, the sea stretched on and on to the horizon and not a ship in sight. Behind, the land lay a patchwork of pastures and bogs and lakes.

Soon, her keen eye picked out a small cottage nestled among some weather-blown bushes about half a mile away.

She had left the house in such a hurry that she had forgotten to eat. A piece of fresh bread appealed to her. Maybe she'd be lucky enough to get a mug of buttermilk also.

It wasn't long before Grainne found herself seated in front of a turf fire with a huge piece of barley bread in one hand and a bowl of warm milk in the other.

Old Maeve lived alone. She was known in the area as the *bandraoi*[4] by some and the *banfheasa*[5] by others. Grainne was unaware of this, but the fact that she was being entertained by a witch or a fortune-teller would not have frightened her anyway. Grainne knew only one fear... the fear of losing her father.   ·

---

[4] *Bandraoi* – witch.

[5] *Banfheasa* – a woman fortune teller.

Maeve seated herself beside Grainne and waited for her to finish her meal. She looked at her for some time before she spoke.

'You'll be an Ui Malley,' she said. 'Aye, "Dubhdarra"'s family.'

'Aye, I am that. I'm Grainne. You'll be knowing my father then?'

'Indeed, I know your father. A great man. And I know your heart is full of love for him.' The old woman chewed on her gums before she spoke again.

Grainne watched her a moment, fascinated by the movement of her lower jaw which was angular and wrinkled, before she answered, 'Yes, I love him very much. He's the king of the seas. I want to be like him.'

Maeve reached for the end of her skirt and wiped the rheum from her small gray eyes. Her black shawl slipped from her head revealing snow-white hair which hung loose about her shoulders. Adjusting the shawl, she again addressed Grainne.

'And so you will, and so you will... But I see many troubles in your future... many enemies... great battles... on land, on sea. You will marry an O'Flaherty... but the love of your life will be... yes, a man coughed up by the sea.

Grainne was about to interrupt. The old hag raised her hand to silence her.

'You will travel in many parts. You will live under the ground. You will be great... very great... Your name will live on and on...'

The old woman fell silent. She started to chew on her gums again.

Grainne spoke: 'Can you tell me about my father?'

Startled, Maeve looked with unseeing eyes at Grainne for a moment.

Grainne thinking she had not been heard, repeated her question.

'You worry for your father's safety. No need, no need at all, at all. I see his life. A long road stretches out before him. He will live to see your children.'

Grainne's heart overflowed with gratitude. She jumped up and threw her arms around old Maeve. 'You've made me so happy. But I don't even know your name.'

''Tis better you don't. Now, I have things to do. Good day to you, Grainne Ui Malley.' So saying the old woman turned her back on Grainne.

Grainne was about to leave. 'Thank you for the food,' she said, 'may I come again?'

'Perhaps,' answered Maeve without turning. She had lost all interest in Grainne. Her mind was on other things.

Leaving the cottage, Grainne realized that there was a very important question she had neglected to ask. How wonderful it would have been to know whether or not she would accompany her father on his next trip to Spain.

But for the answer to that question she would have to wait a whole year.

Chapter Six

Grainne didn't pay too much attention to the words and predictions of old Maeve. The fact that her father would have a long life was all that interested her at the time.

Her mother was occupied with catching up on the local gossip, with entertaining, and visiting relatives and friends. After the first evening, Grainne was not forced to accompany her mother. She was glad to escape all that 'women's cackling,' as her father would say.

She soon found a friend and companion in Rory O'Moore, a lad about her own age. His father owned a number of Connemara ponies and it was Rory's job to exercise them daily.

Grainne was an excellent rider. She had been given a *capalleen*[1] of her own, Finn, on her fifth birthday.

Rory and Grainne spent several hours racing. Unlike Rory, who was racing just for fun, Grainne meant to put her time to good use. She had lost the first prize, by a hand, during the annual spring sports at the Abbey. She had no intention of letting such a thing happen a second time.

---

[1] *Capalleen* – a small horse, a pony.

Towards noon, the two and the ponies were tired out and dirty from head to foot.

'What a sight you are, Grainne Ni Malley!' said Rory, and he laughed when he had led the last pony into the paddock and closed the gate. As he turned to look at her, she had rubbed her face with her muddy hand and all Rory could see behind the dirt was her two large brown eyes.

'You're not much better yourself, Rory O'Moore,' replied Grainne. She tossed her head and started to run towards the sea.

'I'm going for a swim. You can come if you like.'

No sooner had she decided than she had hastened to turn words into action.

'Is it crazed you are, Grainne?' the amazed Rory asked as he stood watching her go.

'Crazed! What do you mean?' she shouted over her shoulder.

'Aren't you afraid of the *Bandia*?[2] She lives out there in the deep parts.' There was fear in his voice.

'What if she does? I'm not her enemy.' Grainne's logic was lost on Rory.

She raced to the water's edge and pulled off her clothes. Dropping them in a heap on a pile of stones, she quickly made her way across the rocks, and before Rory could say another word, she had waded into a shallow pool. She was cautious. She was not a strong swimmer as yet. But, like everything that Grainne put her mind to do, she intended to master that skill before long.

---

[2]   *Bandi* – goddess

Ten minutes later, Grainne emerged blue from the cold Atlantic waters. In her nakedness, she was un-ashamed as Rory stared in amazement.

'What you gawking at? You're a *meatachán*[3], a fraidy cat!' she challenged.

The insult goaded Rory to action. No girl was going to accuse him of cowardice. He lunged toward her and would have struck her had not her quick reflexes enabled her to side step just in time.

As a result, Rory went sprawling on the rocks.

Grainne, still holding her dirty clothes close to her wet body, laughed, a low harsh laugh, a child's version of the 'Dubhdarra' roar.

Before Rory could collect himself, she was far away along the beach. A nymph-like creature, her sallow skin making her one with the kelp, the sand, and the broad dark rocks.

★

The next day the friends made up. Their squabbles forgotten, they spent the morning with the ponies. Later, when Grainne repeated her actions of the previous day, Rory decided that he was not going to let a girl get the better of him. He undressed and challenged the rough waters of the open sea up to the waist, but a swimmer he wasn't – and had no intention of ever becoming one.

They decided to hunt for bird's eggs along the cliffs when they had had enough of the icy waters. As they

---

[3] *Meatachan* – coward.

made their way over the jagged rocks, they came upon a hawk's nest. It seemed to be abandoned. But upon closer inspection, they discovered a small bird had been caught between the rocks. 'Kak, kak,' it cried.

'I think its leg is broken, Rory,' said Grainne as she tried to squeeze her hand between the rocks.

It had always been Grainne's wish to have a falcon of her own. Was she about to get her wish sooner than she expected? Her father had promised to take her on the hunt when she got older. He was a very fine falconer and he swore it was the one sport he would never give up. His lands were particularly suited to the raising and nurturing of these extraordinary birds of prey. Grainne knew the sport had been popular in Ireland for hundreds of years.

'If we can rescue this one, I want to take her home. I saw her first. She's mine.' Grainne was determined.

'Oh, I don't want her. Ach, who cares about an old bird anyway.' Rory said, more angry than hurt. Grainne always wanted to be the chief in everything.

They managed to rescue the bird. Grainne tore a piece of material from her bodice and made a brace to support the broken leg.

They found fresh water in a nearby stream and poured a few drops down the bird's throat. It would live, she concluded.

The next day there was a change in the weather. Dark heavy clouds were gathering low on the horizon. Grainne's thoughts were with her father. She hoped he wouldn't delay too long. She should have been with him. But then, she consoled herself with the thought that he knew just as well as she did that he had only so much time to make it home safely.

The *Faoilan* came swiftly into the bay on the warm breath of the first storm of autumn. But instead of mooring off the shore in her usual place, Owen sailed the ship into one of his secret hideaways.

Grainne was waiting when he set foot on dry land. She was happy to embrace him once again. But she sensed a tension in his actions and his voice: there was something amiss.

She did not want to spoil the joy of the moment, so she decided to wait till they were alone together to ask what it was that troubled her dear father.

It was very late when she finally learned that a Turkish pirate vessel had been seen off the northwest coast, and as if that were not enough, a fleet of English ships, it was rumored, had rounded the coast of Kerry.

'Father, will you have to fight?' Grainne asked.

'I'm sure hoping it won't come to that, a grá. But if we're provoked... An O'Malley never turns his back on an enemy unless he's sure he has the advantage in speed.' He bent and placed a kiss on her forehead. 'But tell me, what have you been doing while I was away?'

Grainne, delighted to have her father's complete attention, gave a full account of her activities.

It was the first time her mother knew exactly what she had been up to. The expression of pain on her lovely face showed her obvious displeasure.

'Grainne! Don't you have any shame? What will people be thinking of you, at all. Don't you have any respect for your family? You have some obligation to give...'

'Margaret, she's only a child. Nobody takes any notice of her. Let her be. Too soon, all too soon her freedom will be a forgotten thing,' Owen told her. He looked at his beloved daughter and his dark eyes betrayed his inner feelings.

'Sure, it won't be long now before we'll have to be looking for a suitable marriage partner. What do you think, Grainne? You want to get married, love?'
They both laughed. The loud, unique, but familiar duet so often heard in Belclare Castle.

★

News came the next day that the Turkish pirates had raided an O'Donnell ship, murdered the crew, and then set fire to the vessel.

When Owen heard the news, he cursed into his beard. His face grew red with anger and for the whole day, he didn't talk to anyone, not even Grainne.

The storm raged for a day and a night. The black waters jumped and leap-frogged and bumped about in the bay. On the stony beach, bundles of kelp and debris were tangled in untidy clumps.

'We'll have an early winter, Grainne,' said her father as the two went to look over the galley and to assess the extent of the damage.

''Tis time we were getting home, I think.' Grainne offered her opinion with the assurance of a veteran seaman.

'You're right, my Sailor Princess. We'll be for Belclare in the morning.'

Chapter Seven

Back home again at Belclare Castle, Grainne and her family resumed their normal activities. Her father, once more, made his rounds checking his buildings and lands. Preparations for the coming winter months were in progress. Fuel – wood and turf – was being stockpiled. Supplies of grain had to be inspected: No sense allowing the mice and rats to get fat on the abundance of autumn's fields. The vegetables still needed to be harvested. Only the parsnips would remain to taste the first frosts of winter. It gave them a good flavor, the housekeeper insisted. The sheep and cattle had been brought home from their summer pastures. They now crowded the meadows and grass lands about the castle, but the barns and pens had to be inspected and refurbished lest a cold winter should force them indoors.

Grainne's mother was busy also. She had to oversee the salting, drying, and smoking of fish, meats, and fruits. Nuts and berries were gathered daily. All must be picked before *Oiche na puca*[1] (Hallowe'en) lest the *puca* spit on them.

There was a sense of urgency about the movements and actions of the servants. The Castle was filled with

---

[1] *Oiche na puca* – night of the spirits.

the spicy odors of plum puddings and barmbracks and honey cakes as the cooks prepared for the upcoming holidays. Hallowe'en was not far off and it would be followed quickly by Christmas preparations.

Grainne wasn't sure which festive time she liked best. She thought perhaps that Oiche na puca might very well be her favorite, because at that time she didn't have to spend half of it in church before getting her presents and being allowed to have fun.

She returned to school in the Abbey. She was the only girl in a class of twenty boys, most of whom were foreign students from France and Spain. Of course, there were always a few English scholars. With these she would rarely have anything to do. Her father had told her enough to know that they were not her friends. Their ships continually attacked her father's vessels.

As usual Grainne was at the top of her class in languages. She got second place in history and geography, but that she was determined to rectify, especially when her opponent was a small boy of the O'Connor Don household.

The foreign boys didn't like the idea of a mere girl getting better reports than they. To prove their superiority, they made fun of her at recess time, calling her names and challenging her to perform feats and skills reserved only for boys and men.

In this way, Grainne learned more than her lessons and became the equal of any boy not only in physical games but also at the gambling table.

One day, Grainne got so mad at one of her tormen-
tors that she challenged him to a duel. The young
Spanish boy, Emmanuel Rojas, gasped at the thought.

'Is your mind really set to do this?' he asked in
disbelief.

'Have you ever known me to run and hide? I'm of
the O'Malley family or have you forgotten?' she
challenged.

'No, no nnnnn,' he stammered. 'But—'

'But, nothing. Meet me tomorrow before school.'

'I'll not draw a sword against a girl. I'll not dishonor
my name and my father's house,' answered the boy.

'No, but you try to dishonor the O'Malley name, a
name older and prouder than yours by hundreds of
years.' Grainne was more than angry, she was furious.

Seeing that no peaceful settlement was going to be
reached, Emmanuel's friends held council.

'This wench, if wench she be...' There was a guffaw
from the group as Richard Cramer, an English boy,
older than the others by several years, made a sugges-
tion.

Grainne didn't hear what he proposed. It took some
time for a consensus of opinion to be reached.

Finally, amid great excitement, they presented their
solution to the problem.

'Instead of fighting with swords, Master Cramer
and the rest of us think the fight should be settled by a
race.' The spokesman for the group was Gabriel
Hernandez. 'A swimming race,' he added.

Grainne thought a moment. As long as she won she
really didn't care. As her father had said, 'An O'Malley
never turns his back on the enemy unless he has the

advantage of speed.' Did she have speed? Well, she'd find out. 'I shall choose the place,' she said, a defiant, crafty glint in her eyes.

It was settled. They would all gather on the beach the following morning.

The sun had a watery smile; the dew was heavy on the grass, and the breakers none too friendly when the children arrived at the appointed time and place.

The contestants stripped. In their excitement about the outcome, the boys forgot the boy-girl part of the quarrel, which had been so important the day before. Now, they were all eager to see who would actually win.

Cramer gave the order to start. 'One, two, three – Go!'

Splash! Grainne hit the waves and battled her way to the rock which marked the distance.

Emmanuel, unaccustomed to the icy waters of the North Atlantic, struggled for a few minutes before he was forced to give up.

The boys, standing on the strand watching him, were angry. He had told them he could swim. He had let them down.

As Emmanuel tried to reach dry land a huge wave struck him. He was thrown off his feet. The waters forced him under. For a moment, he managed to rise above the waves.

'Help! help!' he shouted.

Fortunately, Brother Kevin, a monk from the Abbey was walking in a grove nearby. His morning meditation was interrupted by Emmanuel's cries. He rushed to the shore.

'Glory be to God!' he exclaimed, as he fought the breakers and pulled the half-drowned Emmanuel to the rocks.

As soon as he had caught his breath, Brother Kevin demanded an explanation. Emmanuel tried to speak but his teeth wouldn't stop chattering. His friends had scattered. He felt ill. He had swallowed so much salt water.

Brother Kevin wrapped him in his cloak.

Meantime, Grainne had returned safely to the rocky beach, realizing that there was no one following her.

She had won! She had just finished putting on her clothes when Brother Kevin turned and saw her.

'And what have you to do with the goings on here this morning?'

'It was a fair fight and I won,' she answered.

'This lad almost drowned. Do you know that?'

'Perhaps he couldn't swim,' she said without concern.

'M'Lord Abbot will hear of this.' So saying he lifted the boy into his strong arms and carried him back to the Abbey.

As soon as the morning services were over, the Lord Abbot sent for Grainne.

'Your behavior this morning was most unbecoming, nay shameful.' His stern blue eyes bore into her. She could feel his anger even though his thin pale face did not show any emotion. He adjusted a little cap on the bald spot between two ridges of gray hair, before he continued to speak. 'Your attendance at the classes here in the Abbey must be terminated.'

Grainne interrupted. 'M'Lord Abbot.' But she could not continue as she looked at his pale face and steady piercing eyes.

'I'm sorry,' he continued. 'I've heard good things about you.'

She had never in her life heard him say so much. She met him rarely. On the big feasts of the church he would preside at the services dressed in gold or silver. Then, after the services, he would greet her parents. He might make the sign of the cross on her forehead but his words to her were few.

'Still at the top of your class, Eh? Extraordinary!'

She heard the old priest clear his throat.

'Ahem... don't you have something to say for yourself?'

Grainne had almost forgotten what she had to say. 'Oh, yes.' she replied. It was a fair fight. And I won.'

In spite of himself the Lord Abbot couldn't prevent the smile that crossed his face.

'A fight! I hadn't heard of that! But surely a young lady doesn't fight.'

'Why not? I was only defending my rights,' answered Grainne.

'Perhaps you had better tell me all about this fight. Let's start at the beginning.'

Grainne told her story. Her straightforward manner and clear matter-of-fact account impressed the Abbot of Murrisk.

They discussed the matter at some length. In the end, Grainne convinced the Abbot that she had every right to defend herself. On one point, however, he refused to be moved. She had no reason, in his eyes, for stripping naked before the young men.

Her argument – that it was impossible to swim in long clothes – the Lord Abbot didn't hear or didn't want to hear. At that moment, his only concern was that word of the happening would be noised abroad. His school and all that it stood for would be the laughing-stock of the western world. He had to act. He had to be sure such a thing didn't happen again. He had no other recourse. He would have to inform her father that she could no longer attend the Abbey.

'No, No! I must stay. One day I'll take charge of all my father's ships and lands. I must know. I have to learn.'

The Lord Abbot did not expect this outburst. What child was this? A girl who would take a man's place! 'Extraordinary!' he mumbled, as he stroked his white beard.

But, if the Lord Abbot had decided to expel Grainne, he must have forgotten who it was that held the power in the barony of Murrisk. He had decided without consulting the wishes of Owen 'Dubhdarra' O'Malley.

When Grainne's father was informed of the decision, he immediately held a meeting of all concerned. He was Lord of the region. Nothing would be decided without him.

When all the facts were made known, Owen, instead of being angry with his daughter, was proud of her courage and resolve. She had every right to defend herself, he insisted. Although her method of doing so had been, he confessed, somewhat unusual.

Grainne had to promise to refrain from swimming in future in the general area of the Abbey. And so the matter was settled, and in Grainne's mind her father's stature grew. He was without doubt the most powerful man in all Ireland.

Grainne returned to the Abbey and for a while all went well. She had won the respect of the boys in her class. Some of them even became friendly with her. Her progress was so great that her father could not praise her enough.

Unfortunately, Grainne could not stay out of trouble for long.

Friar Colm, who taught mathematics, was a tall, thin, chisel-faced monk. Grainne had named him 'The Jackdaw.'

One morning 'The Jackdaw' was more ill-tempered than usual. A nasty red bump on his shiny forehead was the reason.

Grainne couldn't resist a snide remark. She turned to Emile who sat next to her, saying, 'Friar Jackdaw has grown a horn.' There was a devilish twinkle in her brown eyes.

'What on earth does she have in her mind? Emile mumbled to himself.

At that moment, Friar Colm chose to ask Emile to solve a problem. Emile had not been listening. Arithmetic was not his most favorite subject.

Grainne saw his embarrassment. She tried to whisper the answer. She wasn't quick enough for Friar Colm, however. His beady gray eyes were riveted on her. His gaunt features seemed more pinched and transparent. He came close to where Grainne was sitting. She knew he didn't like her, but she refused to be frightened by him.

'Yes, it is true what you are thinking,' he said, as if he could read her thoughts. 'Your place is with your mother, at home. You do not belong in this noble institute.' The monk felt a surge of exhilaration in spite of his religious training. He had waited a long time for an opportunity such as this.

'Grainne Ni Malley,' he continued, 'you were prompting.' He paused.

The atmosphere in the room was tense. This was the Chieftain's daughter who was being reprimanded.

The friar continued: 'You were prompting,' he repeated. 'In my class I do not allow prompting. You know that. Yet, you would defy me? Well, Grainne Ni Malley I will show you who is in charge in this classroom... You would be a boy, act as a boy, then, we will treat you as a boy. You will report after school for your punishment.'

There was a gasp of disbelief from Emile. 'No!' was all he managed to say.

Friar Colm turned his attention to Emile.

'So, you also wish to disobey?'

'No, I mean, yes,... I was at fault, not Grainne.'

Grainne stood up. Her brown eyes were unflinching. There was pride, even defiance in her gaze. 'Yes, you are right.' she said. 'I prompted Emile. But, if he wasn't so scared of you he would have been able to answer, himself.'

The blood rushed to the friar's face. For the first time, his students saw color in his countenance. It was an unnerving experience.

Grainne took the caning that evening. Her hands were swollen when she arrived home. She tried to hide them from her father for she believed she deserved the punishment. But when the Lord Owen heard the story, he did not agree. The whole episode had been blown out of all proportions. 'Don't those friars have anything else to do?' he mumbled to himself.

Owen was a practical man. He solved his problems in very practical ways.

Grainne's hands were still sore the next morning. He was not about to allow Friar Colm to have the satisfaction of knowing that he had inflicted such pain on his courageous daughter. Whether or not she was spoiled and undisciplined was a matter of opinion.

Her morning meal finished, Grainne was about to leave for school when her father spoke.

'Grainne, it's that time again! The fishing boats are back and we know how anxious those captains are to part with their fees.' He laughed as he put his hand on her shoulder.

'What say you to our relieving them of their misery?' and he chuckled into his beard.

Grainne's eyes lit up. 'I'm all for that, sir,' she said, saluting her captain, 'I'll be ready in the shake of a lamb's tail.'

She ran to change into her trews. She put on a woolen shift. The weather was turning cold and a sharp westerly plucked the white caps from the swells and flung them high upon the rocks. Her father was right, they would have an early winter.

As she looked for her woolen cap, Grainne also realized how, without saying it, he had saved her from further humiliation at the hands of 'The Jackdaw'!

Father and daughter walked together to the water's edge. Already, his men were at work: calking, patching, sewing ripped sails. It was a busy time.

Since the O'Malleys were primarily a seafaring family, most of the work done near the Castle had to do with shipbuilding, repairing, and with maintaining sea-worthy vessels.

Besides the large galleys and caravels, there were hide-covered coracles and curraghs to be kept, at all times, in good condition. The equipment used, nets, hooks and lines, required constant attention also. Wooden barrels and crates continually needed repair and replacement. There was never a shortage of work. The waters off this western coast abounded with sea life, and fishermen came from many lands to fill their vessels: from England, France, Holland, and even from as far away as Spain and Portugal, they came.

Grainne knew their flags. She learned early to recognize those to be trusted. And, she knew how to drive a hard bargain with those who would cheat her or haggle over the fee she demanded.

She had learned well from 'Dubhdarra.' She outdid him. He might neglect to collect from a small vessel or overlook a meagre catch. Not Grainne; she extracted the last coin. And, if a man were unable to pay, she found other ways to balance his account.

'A tenth of your haul, or nothing,' her voice, an echo of 'Dubhdarra's, rang out. And, from a satchel at her waist, she drew the dice.

So did Grainne add to her father's stocks and her name was known in many lands. In seven languages they called her Grainne, Sailor Princess of The Western Seas.

Chapter Eight

The cold wet days of winter were finally coming to a close. The sun made gallant attempts to smile from behind heavy mists and bad-tempered, driven showers.

Then, in early May, it happened! Spring danced in the fields. Daffodils and cowslips nodded agreeably with the soft breezes. The birds sang sweet love-songs and refused to be quiet till long after the sun had gone to bed. The animals, particularly the cattle and sheep, were busy taking care of their babies.

A time of excitement, activity.

The sea had a different voice and a young look. She had changed her winter gown of black and gray and wore, instead, a robe of greens and blues flecked with diamonds.

Grainne was happy. Things had settled down at the Abbey. She continued to be the best student in her class, but now the boys had accepted her as one of themselves.

Grainne had one brother, Donal, really a stepbrother, who lived at Cathair-na-Mart. Every year he came to pay his father a visit at Belclare.

As he was several years older than Grainne and by nature a timid, shy lad, the brother and sister didn't have much in common.

Donal played the pipes. His music filled the Castle at all hours. In fact, he was such a good musician that he was known as *'Donal-na-Piopa'* (Donal of the Pipes).

Grainne admired his skill and danced to his tunes but she had no interest in learning to play his instrument. Not that she didn't like music but the exercise would keep her indoors too long and that she never liked.

When Donal wrote his songs and poems, Grainne used her quill to calculate weights and measures and the price she could get from the next fishing trip.

On one subject alone, the two were able to speak the same language: falconry.

When Donal was a small boy, Owen, who had no equal in all Connaught, tried to teach him the art of falconry. The boy enjoyed the birds and was fascinated by their spectacular feats. But when it came time to working with them, he was afraid. His father was both disappointed and disgusted with his son.

'What ails you, lad?' Owen yelled at him one day. 'You want to disgrace me before the whole of Ireland?'

'I swear it, Father, 'tis my best effort,' answered Donal.

'Then 'tis a sorry best.' And with that Owen turned his back and walked off.

As a result, Donal knew much of the theory of falconry but little of its practical application.

Grainne's falcon had grown into a fine Peregrine. Her leg had mended beautifully.

'One day, you'll show them all, my Queen,' said Grainne, and stroked Aileen's feathers as the great bird shifted on her perch. Grainne was thinking of the day she would take her pet to join in the hunt with her father. What a glorious occasion that would be, and she was proud to think that she could be the first girl to follow the hunt and to compete as an equal with the men of the area.

Every morning before school she checked to see that all was well with her Aileen. She had joined the family of hawks kept by 'Dubhdarra.' A special cage had been built for her which Grainne, herself, had designed.

During the winter and spring Aileen had grown to her full size. When she spread her wings she covered Grainne's head. She was too big now to rest on her arm, so instead she balanced on her shoulder.

Aileen was a beautiful bird, blue-black feathers above and below a whitish color with gray stripes. She was beginning to gain great strength.

Donal had been several days at the Castle when Grainne invited him to see Aileen in flight. She was so proud of her progress. The long months of training had stood her in good stead. They had told her she had undertaken an impossible task. Her bird was an eyas; there wasn't the ghost of a chance for her to succeed with such a creature.

But Grainne had cast dice with her father. She would challenge any of his Peregrines during the *Booley* hunts next summer.

'Isn't she a beauty?' said Grainne. She talked constantly to the bird.

Donal kept his distance and was silent. His face was a pallid hue.

They had reached a suitable spot, a hill overlooking the whole area. It was an ideal day. The sky was clear blue, only a wisp of cloud over against the great mountain, Croagh Patrick. St. Patrick's mountain where the Saint prayed for forty days and forty nights, asking God's blessing on Ireland and the Irish people.

Gently removing the hood, Grainne allowed the bird to preen for a few seconds. When she had settled down, she undid the jesses.

Aileen remained a second longer, balancing. Then, effortlessly, spreading her great wings, she rose swiftly into the air.

Grainne ran her tongue over her lips. The pride was evident in her dark eyes.

It was a splendid sight.

'You're right, Grainne, she is beautiful! Magnificent!' shouted Donal, impressed.

At first, Aileen did not climb very high; she hovered, as if deciding what to do, then circled the Castle and its surroundings. Finally, using all the power of her mighty wings, she made her ascent, climbing up... up.

Grainne strained to see her. She placed her hand over her eyes to shield them from the unaccustomed glare. As she watched, the bird became a mere speck and then vanished from her sight, lost in the blue beyond.

'Look... look below!' cried Donal. His voice clearly told of his excitement. 'See how the birds rise! Sparrows, blackbirds, even the crows.'

'If they know what's good for them, they'll take cover,' Grainne said matter-of-factly.

'It's said, she's the swiftest creature on earth,' Donal commented. ''Tis hard to believe it. Over a hundred miles an hour. Sure, I'm thinking she's a charmed creature, a fairy spirit, who else could have such power?'

Grainne, ever alert, awaited the supreme moment.

The peregrine was soaring now within sight. They could see the great span of her wings as she glided, feigned stoops, arose, soared, played the fool.. How she relished her freedom!

'See how she plays. Flying for the love of it. Queen of the skies.'

And in her mind Grainne thought, *As I will be Queen of the Seas*.

'I've a mind she'll kill today,' said Donal.

'Oh yes, but she's particular. She'll not choose the grouse in the meadow. Nor will she pick the weak. No, only the strong. Only the leader of the covey for her.' Grainne declared proudly. And again her mind filled with images of fleeing pirate ships... ships pursued by her galleys. And she knew she would be particular, choosing only the Captain's ship, the one which held the richest loot, the greatest treasure, to rob and plunder.

Then it happened.

They saw a brief glimpse of Aileen upside down, her deadly talons stretched.

'She missed!' cried Donal.

But no sooner had he spoken than she was again in pursuit, above this time. In that position the talons struck and the grouse dropped from the sky and was instantly followed by the hawk.

Grainne was wild with excitement. She danced and twirled and shouted. Then remembering her brother, she said, 'Let's be sitting a while. Aileen will take her time now, cleaning, eating, playing; she won't return till she's good and tired.'

'You've accomplished much with that bird, Grainne. Did you tell me she is an eyas falcon?'

'Yes, indeed. Found her in the rocks last time we went to Moher O'Malley country. Fortunately, I happened on her before she starved to death.'

'Do you think she might come to me?' asked her stepbrother. For one moment, Donal aspired to the challenge. It looked so easy.

'I'm not sure. She's never gone to anyone but me,' Grainne answered.

'Perhaps if I just stood here.' He got up and took a position on a rise of ground. Then he changed his mind and took his stand on the highest part of the hillock, holding his arm out.

Grainne hesitated. 'It would be a first. Are you sure you really want to?' she asked.

Donal wasn't sure but he couldn't back down now. Allow a mere girl and a child to best him? 'Sure, I'm sure.' he said, a sting in his voice.

'We'll see what her mood is when she returns.'

It was over an hour later when Grainne's keen sight spotted the hawk.

She was circling high overhead. Seeking her mistress.

Donal took up his position. But the hawk kept circling. She had no intention of landing on a stranger's arm.

'She'll not come in,' said Grainne. 'You can stand there all night, but she'll not come to you.'

'Oh, very well. If she's that particular.' His scowling face showed his displeasure.

'You have knowledge of these hawks yourself, Donal,' was all Grainne said as she stood on the high ground where, immediately, Aileen swooped down to her shoulder.

Donal was peeked. 'We try tomorrow,' he suggested. Only this time, I'll release her so she knows me better.' He tried to assure himself that all was not lost. He would show Grainne who was the better falconer.

Again Grainne hesitated, saying, 'You know it takes longer than that for a hawk to trust...'

But Donal interrupted. He was determined. 'I know what I'm doing,' he said, gruffly. Mayhap, he wanted to impress his father, or wanted to show his little sister that he was a man, and that if she could control a bird, he most certainly could do so. It was only a matter of allowing the hawk to get used to him.

Next morning, because he was a guest, Grainne agreed to take Aileen out again.

They chose a spot not too far from the Castle, where they intended to practice for a while allowing Aileen to get used to Donal.

Arriving at the place, Grainne handed the bird rather reluctantly to Donal.

'Easy now, Aileen. Donal will let you go in a moment. Easy girl.' Grainne said, continuing to soothe and encourage the hawk.

As soon as she was settled on Donal's arm, Grainne removed the hood. The bird looked around. She was clearly frightened. She tried to go to Grainne's shoulder but lost her footing.

Suddenly, she rose into the air, her jesses trailing.

'Oh, no!' was all Grainne could say. She placed her hands over her mouth as if to suppress a scream. She watched. She waited. She hoped...

'Aileen,' she called, 'Aileen come.' Grainne pleaded. 'No, not there.' The bird was dangerously near a clump of trees.

Grainne ran to try to warn her, 'No Aileen, no!' she cried.

The bird swerved at the sound of Grainne's voice.

The jesses tangled impeding her ability to land. She struggled, she splayed her magnificent wings trying to balance.

In seconds the bird's neck was broken.

Grainne stood in horror looking at her beautiful pet as she lay in the heather in front of her, a lifeless heap, her intelligent head thrown to one side.

'I'm sorry. It was all my fault,' Donal said. He had failed again. He really felt ashamed and humiliated and his face was a deep red color.

Grainne said nothing. She was too near to tears, but she would not cry. She had gone against her better judgment. She had allowed herself to be talked into doing something she knew couldn't work.

It was a hard lesson that Grainne learned that day. But it was one which stood her in good stead in the years to come.

She would never again allow her heart to rule her head.

Chapter Nine

Summer came. Long days bursting with smells and sounds and sunshine.

It was *Booley* time!

'Don't touch that!' Margaret warned Grainne. She was hot and tired and had just finished packing the last hamper of food.

The smell of fresh baked breads escaped from between the loosely woven reeds as baskets were piled one on top of another.

Bunches of vegetables, onions, carrots, cabbages, garlic, turnips, and parsnips, and stacks of pungent herbs were ready waiting for the creels.

Bed-sheets and white woolen blankets were wrapped in coarse linen sacks. Margaret's wooden bathing basin, which had been stored since the previous year, was filled with many of her special soaps and toiletries. All was ready.

It was a sign to everyone that the O'Malley household was about to leave Belclare Castle and move for several weeks to the hills for a *Booley* (summer living).

Grainne was familiar with the proceedings. She knew that as soon the workmen arrived at the prearranged spot, they would erect a large, one-room, wooden house. The roof was thatched with rushes.

The ground within covered with the same sweet-smelling reeds.

This was the time when The O'Malley and his household left the Castle to graze his herds of cattle. It was also a time for fishing in cool running streams and freshwater lakes. And Owen took advantage of the long leisurely evenings to negotiate with far-flung families about future orders; goods from his voyages or his plunder.

These were the days when Grainne was free to explore the hills. She could take her capalleen, Finn, into the gulleys and across the most rugged ridges. She often stopped to taste the wild strawberries or to gather bouquets of flowers: figwort; eyebright, yellow rattle, and toadflax. And, clinging to stony outcroppings, she frequently found what she called 'summer bells.' And, when she reached the higher ground, she would shout for the sheer joy of it. She would listen for the echo of her own voice as it mocked her in the valley below.

In those long summer days, Grainne ran barefoot through lush dewy grasses and purple heathers. She searched for wild birds and spent hours with her falcon – a magnificent creature given her by her father to replace Aileen.

Then, when his work was done, she watched the hunt from an elevated ridge and longed for the day when she could accompany him in his favorite sport.

She never ceased to admire 'Dubhdarra' as he rode out on his black stallion at the head of the party. While at his heels, awaiting his command to start the chase, eighteen to twenty wolfhounds collected.

Grainne knew her father's lands stretched over a vast area and consisted of several different types of terrain, from the rich farm land near Belclare Castle, to large expanses of marsh and bogland, and everything in between; undulating hills, rough mountainous areas, and thick wooded places. And over these sparsely populated lands roamed wolves, deer, fox, and badgers, while soaring aloft the black eagle lorded it over the barnacle goose, the woodcock, gannet, and cormorant. And in the crystal lakes the stately swans seem to float upon the quiet waters.

From these well stocked lands, the elk and deer were the favorite of Owen O'Malley. The excitement of a successful hunt and the anticipation of tasty venison for supper added to the festive atmosphere.

The feasting would last for several hours, during which time, the entire animal was roasted. It was eaten with oaten cakes and a variety of vegetables. There was plenty of ale, wine, whey, sweet milk, and buttermilk to drink at all times.

The whole assembly gathered later to spend time around the huge fire which burnt far into the night. And, under star-filled skies, they listened as a *seanchai*[1] or their own bard told them stories of their ancient heroes, and heroines.

Grainne closed her eyes as she lay on the soft grass. Her father stretched out beside her. The lilt of the story-teller's voice and the rhythmic meter of the poem cast their spell on all.

---

[1] *Seanchai* – story-teller

A foreign guest might well have asked if everyone was asleep. But this was a spiritual moment. Great lessons were learned as the story-teller told his tale, and Grainne missed nothing.

"Tis a good place and time you've chosen for the telling of "The Tain Bo Cuailgne,"[2] she spoke to the Seanchai, old Liam, from the woods yonder.

And as he pulled his well worn bratt about him, he answered, 'Nothing escapes you, Grainne Ni Malley,' and winked at her father with a turn of his head.

She knew it was a compliment. And, when her father nodded in agreement, she smiled.

The days of the *Booley* followed each other in sweet serenity that summer of 1539. Fat lazy days, for the most part, for family and servants. A time of enjoyment and indulgence in nature's abundance.

But everything has an end. Only three, carefree, leisurely days remained before all the packing would begin again and it would be time to return to the Castle.

It was an unusually warm evening. The family meal had been prepared. It was ready to serve as soon as Owen made his appearance.

Grainne, always late, came running into the house.

'Where's father?' she blurted. There was a wild fear in her eyes and terror in her voice.

'He's out with the hounds. What ails you, child?' asked her mother seeing her stricken face.

---

[2] 'Tain Bo Cuailgne' – 'The Brown Bull of Cuailgne' from ancient Irish mythology.

Grainne could only utter the word 'Fire!' as she sped.

As soon as Owen O'Malley heard Grainne's frantic story, he called his men. Within five minutes, he was galloping at the head of a small army in the direction of Belclare Castle.

Grainne was angry when her father told her that she couldn't go with him. She felt she could be useful in some way. And she fought back the tears and wished for the umpteenth time that she were a boy.

'I'll carry water. I'm faster than anyone else.'

She knew she mustn't delay her father with her insistence. So she stepped aside when he shouted, 'Out of the way, a grá. You'll be safe here,' and galloped off.

She didn't want to be safe, especially if he was in danger.

Her father was scarcely a mile away, when she decided that she couldn't just wait for hours with a group of frightened women. She had to do something. She *would* do something.

She mounted a horse and set off after the men.

The flames were leaping high in the Bay when Grainne descended to the flat lands surrounding the Castle. Under cover of some trees, she drew near the workhouses. These buildings and sheds, so far, were safe. She was thankful for that.

As she crept closer, she could hear the sounds of battle and hear the cries of the wounded.

She prayed for her father. 'Sweet Jesus take care of him.'

The smell of burning oakum and timber reached her nostrils. She could see a cloud of black smoke hanging over the Bay.

She needed a weapon of some kind. Her first thought was the tool-shed. But she changed her mind because so many were too heavy for her to handle. A knife!

Making her way to the kitchen, Grainne discovered Bridget, the old serving woman, lying near the turf fire.

'My God! Oh no!' She knelt down and looked carefully. Perhaps she was still alive... Where were the other servants, she asked herself.

Bridget moved.

Then Grainne saw it... a nasty gash at the back of her head. She must stop the bleeding. She pulled a white towel from a rack hear the fire and rolled it into a ball. Kneeling again, she pushed it against the wound.

'I must get help.' she cried. Grainne was frantic.

She ran outside. She searched in several huts and workhouses before she finally found three servants huddled together in the peat shed.

'Come, come quickly. Bridget needs help!' she ordered the servants.

At first, the women were too frightened to move.

'Are you coming or do I have to tell Father you refuse?' she shouted.

At the mention of her father, the servants thinking the Master was in the Castle, jumped up and followed her.

Grainne returned to the kitchen. She grabbed a knife and holding it in front of her, she quietly tiptoed from room to room, searching to make sure there was no one else in the Castle.

She was about to leave, when she thought she should check the cellar. A good place to hide, she told herself.

Now, holding the knife in both hands, Grainne slipped noiselessly down the stone steps to the cellar. In the darkness, it was difficult to see. But she could hear a gasping sound followed by a moan not too far off.

Slowly, deliberately, she felt her way. As she reached the bottom step, she suddenly stopped.

A man!

Had she moved another inch, she would have stepped on him.

He was lying huddled on the stone floor and he seemed to be in great pain. She must be cautious. At that point, Grainne couldn't see well enough to know whether he was friend or foe.

She waited a moment, not daring to breath.

What should she do? She felt a shiver run through her body. It was cold and damp in the cellar but Grainne didn't feel the cold or the damp. She had to make a decision and fast.

The man moved. He mumbled something. The words were incoherent.

Grainne waited... If he but said a few more words, she would know what to do, she thought.

The seconds seemed hours.

Again, the man muttered. Grainne caught the words, 'Bastards... all of 'em.'

English! The enemy lying at her feet! He must be the one who almost killed poor old Bridget. Well, he'd probably try to kill her too if...'

He moved.

Grainne could feel the warmth of his breath. She drew back.

'Someone there?' he cried out. There was fear in his voice.

'Aye, there's someone here,' Grainne answered in her native language.

'A child! Hah!' he exclaimed, and laughed, a half laugh.

Her father's words rang in her brain, 'A wounded boar strikes again.'

Grainne waited no longer. Raising the knife high above her head, she plunged it down with all her might.

She heard a long low scream. A gurgling sound, then a grasping grating of fingernails on the flag floor.

She turned and ran up the steps and out of the Castle.

For a long time, she balanced herself against the cold granite wall. She felt sick. She had to find her father.

Grainne didn't know how she got to where her father was. Hair flying and spattered with blood, she threw herself into his arms.

Owen dropped the water bucket. The fires on board his flagship were under control.

They clung to each other for some moments before he spoke.

'Grainne, *mo stóirín*.'[3] he said, looking into her dark eyes, 'Tell me. Tell your father.'

'I killed him. He tried to kill Bridget.'

'You what?' said Owen, aghast. 'I told you to stay... Did he hurt you?'

'No, he was hurt, Father. I was afraid he'd...' She buried her head against her father's chest and sobbed, big deep sobs without tears, until the horror faded, and she could feel, only, his strong warm arms about her.

When he was assured that she hadn't been touched, he kissed her and hugged her closer.

'My brave daughter,' was all he could say.

★

Owen lost two men and four curraghs that day. The fight ended when the enemy was driven into the sea. None escaped the swords of 'Dubhdarra' O'Malley and his followers.

It had been Grainne's quick thinking and keen eyes that had saved her father's ships and their Castle home on that summer evening of 1538.

---

[3] *Mo stóirín* – my treasure

Chapter Ten

Grainne had always been tall for her age. But since her ninth birthday, she had grown at least another inch. She looked older than she really was.

Owen had promised that she would accompany him on his next trip to Spain and Portugal.

It had been a long hard fight. She had pestered, coaxed, and cajoled. Owen had been pulled back and forth; his decision to take her along was not an easy one. Margaret, he knew, had valid, logical objections to the whole idea.

At first, she voiced her disapproval by loud protestations. 'It's unseemly, unthinkable, what a childish idea!' She blamed Owen for permitting the notion to even take shape in Grainne's mind. 'You've indulged this child's every whim ever since she could toddle. Now, it's too late for me to have any influence on her.' She sighed. 'What will become of her?' Margaret was upset, worried.

'Grainne is strong in body and mind. She's intelligent. She'll always be her own woman,' said Owen.

'Aye, an' that's the problem. Strong willed and stubborn as she is now, what will she be in a few years time? No man, in his right mind, would have her to wife.'

Owen laughed. 'Aye, she'll be a handful, that I'll grant you,' he said.

Margaret, thinking she was having some effect on Owen, continued; 'She's completely lacking all feminine graces. She moves, no, she leaps from one place to another like a wild uncultured lad. Her manners are appalling, her language coarse and loud...'

Owen had enough. 'Well, my dear, you've made your point. Grainne is all mine.' So saying, he turned and left the room. He was disturbed. *Dar Dia!* Grainne! he said to himself, why weren't you a boy?

As he went about his work, he couldn't help but think of Margaret's words. Had he really made a bad decision? It wasn't too late, he could always come up with some excuse or another not to take her. But then, as he reconsidered, it would surely break her poor wee heart. And besides, he was looking forward to having her along with him. Owen bit his lip. 'Twas a hard thing he had to do. No matter what he decided he would hurt one or other of his loved ones.

Meantime, Grainne's every waking hour was occupied with thoughts of the upcoming voyage.

At last, at last I'll see Spain! she told herself. Her imagination ran away with her. In her history classes, she had learned that her ancestors, the Milesians, coming directly from Spain, had invaded Ireland at about 1000 BC. Led by the inspired bard, Amergin, the first Gaelic people eventually conquered the whole island of Inisfail, Isle of Destiny, as it was then called.

So Grainne felt, deep down, that she was in reality making a pilgrimage to the land of her forefathers.

She imagined she could taste the wine fruit, her father had described. She dreamed of picking the delicious fruits he had so often brought home for her: oranges, grapefruit, lemons, and limes.

Who could tell what else she might see. The great city of Cordova! She knew it had been transformed into a place of exquisite beauty by the Moors who had come to Spain in AD 711.

She couldn't wait to get started. To be on her way, to be on the wide open sea, only the sky above and the rolling waters beneath her. To be alone with her beloved father day and night for many weeks to come. It was all she could do to keep from shouting in her hoarse voice, shouting for joy.

Preparations for the voyage had been stepped up. There were rumors of Turkish pirate ships off the coast of Donegal. Owen wanted to avoid, if at all possible, any clash with those murdering foreign devils. A decision was made to leave a week earlier than planned.

Grainne heard the discussions and disagreements between her parents. Always they had the same conclusions: her mother stressing the fact that it was not fitting for a little girl to be in the company of rough sailors day in day out, for six to eight weeks; her father making the point that it would be easier now than later. The men looked on her as a child. 'There wasn't one o' them that wouldn't give his life for her,' she heard her father say.

Why wasn't I born a boy? she asked herself. *I could go anywhere, do anything, no one would say a word.* Then, in her practical way, she concluded, *Well I'm a girl. I'll always be a girl, and I'm not going to let that stop me.*

The arguments between her parents continued. If only there was something she could do to convince both of them that she could be just as much a part of the crew as Brien, the ship's boy.

She pondered the problem for several more days. Time was running out. The caravels were loaded, the galleys ready. They would sail on the morning tide, God willing, she heard her father tell the crew.

Grainne, sitting on a barrel of salted fish, was watching the last-minute preparations. Young Brien ran past carrying a coil of rope. He was so busy, he hadn't time to talk to her. She noticed his bare feet and torn trews. He looked cold and thin. He even seemed small.

Grainne stood up. She called to him. 'Brien, Brien wait.' She caught up with him. Then standing close beside him, she realized she was indeed taller, by at least two inches!

'I'm bigger than you,' she said.

'So! You're bigger than me. One day I'll be bigger than you. Boys are always bigger than girls,' he countered with assurance.

'Ha, well right now is all that matters,' answered Grainne. In her mind there was no earthly reason why this 'shrimp' should go to sea and she be denied. She was stronger, bigger and...as she sought for other comparisons the idea struck her.

She knew what she had to do. She took off on swift legs for home.

Brien stood looking after her, his mouth wide open. He shook his head. 'Women,' he mumbled. Not understanding her actions, he recalled the words of his shipmates, 'Who knows a woman's mind? Sure, 'tis easier to know the bottom of the sea than the thoughts of a female.' he told the circling gulls.

Grainne didn't hear his remarks, nor did she care. She had a job to do.

Instead of going into the Castle, she ran around the side and slipped quietly into the tool-shed. She saw the neat rows of sickles, saws, flails and scythes.

'Where are the sheep shears?' she asked herself. She was sure they were kept with all the other tools. Yes, several empty spaces on the wall clearly marked the spots intended for the shears.

She looked around. Not a sign of them anywhere. Then she remembered, that at this time of year, the shears were carefully cleaned and greased. They would not be needed again till the warmer days of spring when the sheep would lose their winter coats. What could she do now? There was no other way. She would have to go into the Castle and take the small scissors her mother used. She ran the risk of being caught and stopped.

It was getting late. Her father would be home soon. She must hurry. It was up to her, she knew, to tilt the balance in her favor.

Her beloved father was still wavering. It was a big decision. He wanted to do whatever was best for her, but he had her mother to please, also.

Grainne had to gamble. She had to take a chance.

Fortunately, her mother was occupied with the cooks in the kitchen. News of the early departure had been received and now there was a scramble to prepare as much cooked food as possible.

Grainne seized the opportunity. She slipped into her parents' bedroom and found the scissors lying beside some embroidery.

Quickly, she hid it inside her bodice and made her way back outside the Castle. She ran to a clump of bushes. There hidden from view, she slowly and deliberately started to cut off her beautiful, long, black hair. When, finally, she could feel little or no hair left on her head, she decided the job was done.

She stood before her parents, a small, very determined little girl, with fists clenched and mouth firmly set. Her large brown eyes blazed with defiance.

There was silence. For several moments both parents were speechless.

'I have to go! I must, I must!' said their young daughter. 'I'm bigger and stronger than Brien. I can be a ship's boy better than he.' Her eyes looked larger and seemed to bulge in their sockets as she made her point.

Grainne watched her mother's reaction. To her amazement, her mother was strangely quiet. Perhaps, she wasn't feeling well. Her pretty blue eyes grew bigger and bigger. Her face became quite pale and she started to reach for her father's arm.

Her father, her quick eye detected, had tried to smother what should have been a loud boisterous laugh, in a fit of coughing.

As soon as he had control of himself, Owen turned to his wife, Margaret. By this time, she had found her tongue; but seeing the twinkle in his eyes and his poor attempt at concealing his real feelings, Margaret's nerves became unstrung. She broke down and sobbed.

'*Dar Dia!*' Grace muttered. Why did her mother take on so, she asked herself. It was now perfectly clear to her why the menfolk didn't want women to accompany them on their business trips.

Grainne had often seen her mother's reactions, but she never ceased to be amazed. In her opinion, they were quite unnecessary and without reason.

Her father, on the other hand, took everything in his stride. He usually saw the humorous side of a situation first. He never reacted without giving the matter cool calculated thought.

Grainne awaited her sentence. Like a criminal brought to justice, she felt the weight of her guilt, but she felt no compunction.

'Sure 'tis no great catastrophe, my love.' said Owen. 'The wee lass wanted so much to go on this trip.' He could no longer suppress a smile. 'Whoever would have thought she'd do it,' he whispered to himself. 'There's no stoppin' my Sailor Princess when her mind is made up.' There was a glint of admiration in his eyes. The child has spunk, he thought.

'Come Grainne,' he said, holding out his arms. 'Come my little '*Granuaile*' (bald Grainne). If you were willing to part with your beautiful hair, then I'll not be denying you, lass.' He pressed her to his heart. 'You'll be the Captain's boy.'

That was the first time in Grainne's life that a tear escaped. It ran quickly down her cheek. She was glad no one saw it. As she nestled close to her father's warm heart, a great sigh of relief was all he heard.

Owen turned his attention to his wife once more. Her face had, in that short space of time, changed color several times, from a pale pink to a blushing rose. Behind her flashing blue eyes, a raging fury was desperately trying to burst forth.

As far as her mother was concerned, Grainne knew she might as well go sit with the chickens for the rest of the evening. There would be no peace in the Castle.

Her father spoke. 'Sure, there's no use in fretting, Margaret, darling. What's done's done. 'Twill grow again. I'm thinking, by the time we return she'll look halfway human.'

Chapter Eleven

The *Santa Cruz*, flagship of Owen 'Dubhdarra' O'Malley was a three-masted Portuguese caravel. The stern of the ship was square as was the great topsail.

It had a high poop deck and forecastle. This new caravel carried a few guns below deck. It was not a very big ship but it was fast. And that's what Owen liked most about it.

The sleeping quarters for the Captain were below the forecastle and were really cramped.

Every inch of the ship was packed with cargo. Forty men were also crammed on board and had to sleep wherever they could find a spot to lie down.

To be a sailor on Owen's ships, a man had to be able to do almost any job he was asked to do. One day, he might have to repair a sail or make a rudder. The next, he could be called upon to cook or forge a metal part.

One of the most important duties of the ship's boy was to turn the hourglass. This job was accompanied by a chant and took place each half hour; it was a monotonous job and one which would not have suited Grainne's temperament one jot, no matter how much she had bragged about her being a better ship's boy than Brian.

She could barely see the flagship as she hastily dressed in the early hours of that late September morning in 1539.

An odd collection of vessels were anchored close by in the Bay. Galleys and long boats sitting low in the water were surrounded by curraghs and small sailing-ships. These latter would sell their cargoes of meats and fish to the larger Irish cities of Galway, Limerick, and, if necessary, Cork. Then, they would return home leaving the bigger vessels to proceed to the Continent.

Grainne's heart was pounding. She must be very careful not to do anything, in the next hour, which would change her father's mind.

Her mother came into her room. She was all teary-eyed. She blew her nose in a fine linen kerchief.

Grainne felt a lump come into her throat.

'Are you wearing your new woolen shift? It will be cold on that ship,' she said, and her voice was soft and full of concern.

'Yes, Mother. Don't worry, I'll be fine.'

Margaret looked anxiously a moment at her little daughter. How quickly she was growing up! Her cropped hair was a sight. But she wouldn't say any more about it.

'Be sure you stay close to your father at all times.' Then she said, throwing her arms around her, 'Know that I love you very much, my Grainne. 'Tis true, I scold you and try to teach you the ways of a lady but...'

Grainne knew her mother would begin to cry. She just couldn't bear a scene at this time.

'Mother, I'll be fine, don't worry,' was all she could say. Then she pulled away.

She quickly covered her head with a woolen cap. Her mother's tears, she felt, were, in part, caused by her shorn locks. 'You'll want to talk to father before he leaves,' she said, trying to distract her.

Breakfast was not a happy time. Grainne was glad to be out of the Castle and on her way. She felt free... just as she knew the hawk, Aileen, had felt when she used to lose herself in the endless blue of a summer sky.

The sun's rays were now visible behind the Abbey. Grainne stood beside her father on the boat's prow, proud and bursting with happiness as the flotilla set sail.

It was her first trip in the new caravel. She had never seen Clew Bay from such a vantage point. She always knew there were islands, too many to count in the Bay, but today there seemed to be even more. Some looked like clay pots turned upside down and not much bigger. Others, she realized, were large enough to support huge herds of fine cattle. And all belonged to her father, 'Dubhdarra', Chief of Murrisk.

As the *Santa Cruz* wound its way to the ocean, she pointed out, to her father, the places where she fished for silver herring and the shallows where she learned to swim and sail the lovely gift he had brought her from Spain.

Leaving the Bay behind, they set out into the mighty Atlantic.

There was a brisk wind. The sea was calm and had a sparkle in its smile. It would be a good run, easy sailing to Galway.

The hills of Connemara and The Twelve Bens were to their left.

'The lands of the O'Flaherty.' Owen pointed as he spoke.

Grainne knew that this great family was tied to her own through marriage, as well as through feuding and death, for hundreds of years.

Suddenly, she remembered the words of Old Maeve. 'You will marry an O'Flaherty.' She didn't much care for the idea just then. But her practical mind did note that O'Flaherty land was close to her father's... more land, more ships, more power.

'Father, will I have to get married?' she asked suddenly.

'Well now, that's a strange question. A girl doesn't have to, but 'tis a good thing. Most women want children. But what brought all this on?'

'Oh nothing. I was just thinking,' she replied. Grainne didn't tell her father everything.

Galway, the 'City of the Tribes', was so named because in the fourteenth century, fourteen prominent Norman families settled there. In time, it became a powerful walled city built by its merchant inhabitants. Into the glorious Galway Bay, Grainne and her father sailed in the late afternoon.

Galway was known as a great trading port from the Baltic to the Mediterranean. Its large exports of wool, linen, animal skins and leathers, fish and meats as well as lampreys and lime, were the city's main source of wealth.

Owen O'Malley knew he would be asked to pay a fee for the privilege of selling his goods in the city.

He also knew he and his vessels would be suspect. He was a Gaelic Lord; his speech, clothing, and appearance were very different from these city people.

But if the Galway merchants didn't like his looks or understand his language, they were always glad to make a profit from his well stocked vessels.

It was the first time that Grainne had ever been to the big city. Although, she was filled with anticipation, she hardly knew what to expect.

So many people in so small an area! So much hustle and bustle. The houses all crowded together. The noise!

'Father, it's impossible! How can people live here?' she cried.

Her father laughed his deep bass laugh. 'I can see, you'll not become a city lass, then.'

'Not, if I'd have to live like a chicken in a coop.' She definitely wasn't impressed.

At first she didn't care to go ashore, but then whiffs of roasting sausages and other tantalizing odors reminded her that she hadn't eaten since early morning.

'Let's see how their sausages taste,' she said finally. There was a mischievous glint in her dark eyes. 'Can Brien come, too?'

'Sure, call the lad.'

Brien was glad to accompany Grainne and her father, and he was happy to have someone his own age to talk to.

Grainne and Brien had become good friends now that they had to live together on board the *Santa Cruz*.

They played cards and Grainne taught him chess. They threw dice and fought over small objects.

She relieved him at his job, taking care to be accurate when turning the hourglass. She would watch for the last grain of sand and then bellow in her raspy voice the chant Brien had taught her:

One o'clock and all's well
The winds are fair. The devil in hell.
Swells look fine, sails look good
And thank you, God, for our daily food.

A freckled-faced lad with a head of auburn curls, Brien was an orphan. He had dancing blue eyes and a pretty face for a boy. He was quick and nimble. And no one, other than Grainne, could outrun him.

His parents had been killed in a raid upon their island home on Inishturk.

Shortly after, Owen had taken him into his employ. He had been sailing the high seas for two years now and had proved to be a reliable ship's boy.

'Come on, you two,' said Owen, who was also feeling hunger pangs.

Permission was granted to the crew to go ashore. As long as a few men remained at all times to guard the ships, the others were free.

Grainne and Brien enjoyed the savory foods: sausages, puddings, black and white; sweetmeats and cakes. They both stuffed themselves and then washed the lot down with a mug of sweet milk.

Leaving a sidestreet, they came to a large open area. There were neat cobblestones under foot, and they were in the market-place. Stalls and booths of every shape and color were set out in long rows.

The din was chaotic. The crowds pushed and shoved. Grainne was unaccustomed to such close contact. She wanted to bolt, to fly to some wide open space, to be free.

Then her attention was drawn to a live performance.

Upon an elevated platform, men and young boys were shouting at one another in the harsh English tongue. Some turned cartwheels, mimicked, poked fun at each other, or members of the audience, in knavish gestures foreign and rude. There was no harp to accompany their line, no attempt to make their words rhyme or sing.

Grainne was bored. Although she understood most of what they were saying, she did not find the show amusing. They did not speak of the great feats of ancient heroes and heroines but only of common ordinary happenings, coarse jokes, and other foolishness.

'I've had enough of Galway, Father.' she said, 'let's go back to the ship. There's more room there,' she laughed.

'I'd like to get a gift for your mother before we leave.' Owen turned down a sidestreet in search of a trinket stall.

They soon came to a jeweler's shop. Inside, an old man was hunched over a beautiful, gold neckband. He was carefully engraving the face of the lunula[1] with criss-crossed lines.

---

[1] *Lunula* – ancient Celtic neckband.

'How much for the piece?' Owen asked in his native tongue.

For a moment the man was startled. '

Eh? Well,' he hesitated. He hadn't forgotten his heritage, but years of speaking a foreign language had thrown him off guard.

'Well,' he said, searching for the correct words, 'for you M'Lord, a mere nothing,' he chuckled. 'Sure, 'tis an honor to be serving you M'Lord...' He waited for Owen to introduce himself and then he continued, 'Ah ha! A greater honor I haven't had for many a long day.'

Grainne watched and listened. The two haggled back and forth until a mutually acceptable price was arrived at.

Owen made his purchase, had it wrapped in a silk covering and concealed it in an inner garment next to his heart.

As they went through the alleys back to the ship, Brien whispered to Grainne. 'I want to buy you a neckband when we get to Spain.'

'Look at me, Brien; 'tis teasing me you are,' she replied. 'Do I look like the kind of girl to wear a neckband? I thank you for your kind thought, though, Brien.' Grainne then pulled off her cap.

'What do you think, now?' she said with a curtsey. 'Kind sir, hand me my gold fibula for I would fasten my cloak against the winter gale.'

They both laughed and Brien understood how Grainne was and did not take offense.

The *Santa Cruz* and the other larger ships pulled out to sea on the next tide. The smaller vessels would return home as soon as they had disposed of their cargoes.

Sailing due west, Owen reached the Aran Islands, then he set a south- westerly course.

Grainne had fallen asleep and didn't wake till the splashing waters off the forked Kerry coast were left behind.

She looked around. The sun was climbing out of bed and she knew by its ruddy face that there was a change in the weather. 'So you show a sudden temper and would tell us of your mood,' she said addressing the scarlet ball.

All around her the sea stretched on and on to meet the sky. Where did one end and the other begin? She ran from one part of the ship to the other. This was a new experience. Always before, she had been able to see some land. But now it was sea and sky, sky and sea and nothing else.

Only the sounds of the black waters as they sloshed against the ship's side or the cries of the men as they went about their chores. It was a vast and awesome place and Grainne felt very small indeed.

But for all that, her heart sang. It sang with the lapping waters and the blowing breezes, with the flapping sails and the tap, tap, tap of the ropes against the masts.

Grainne was not afraid. She was a child of the sea. And as she stood upon the prow, she spread her arms wide as if to embrace its vast expanse.

Her father looking at her, at that moment, realized more than ever before that his daughter was no ordinary child. She was born to greatness. She was destined to rule. She was indeed a worthy guardian of the O'Malley motto:

'*Terra Marique Potens* – Powerful by Land and Sea.'

Chapter Twelve

The Bay of Biscay was not Owen's favorite place, particularly in a storm.

They had been five days at sea. The evening was calm, too calm. Not a puff of wind. The *Santa Cruz* and the other caravels had made little or no headway for over four hours.

'We're in for it, I'm thinking,' said Owen to Grainne as he studied the skies.

'I can feel it too, Father.'

He gave the order to lower the sails.

Within the hour, heavy black clouds had gathered on the horizon. Soon the winds picked up. At first, they played with the waves, but all too soon a fight began. The waves grew angrier and the winds fought back, hurling and whipping until both were furious with each other. Soon the fight became a battle: a fierce battle, one seeking to show the other which was the stronger and better fighter.

The ships were tossed about and couldn't be controlled. There was nothing Owen could do in the face of such awesome rage.

'Best you go below, a grá,' Owen said to Grainne. 'This is not going to let up for a long time.'

Grainne wanted to stay. A peal of thunder seemed to shake the very foundations of the earth far under the towering waters. Great flashes of lightning appeared to torch the sea from end to end. A magnificent sight! She would remember this display until her dying day. It was her first real storm at sea and the elements were doing their very best to impress her.

As she dallied, her father's voice rang out, 'Go below, at once.' His voice was stern. He had never spoken to her before like that.

She would not cause him any undue worry. Quickly, she dropped into the forecastle, but she made sure to settle herself where she could see not only her father but much of what was going on outside also.

It was about midnight and Grainne had fallen asleep. Owen was still at the helm. Young Brien had just turned the hourglass. His small voice wasn't heard above the howling of the gale.

He left his post to relieve himself. At that moment a tremendous towering wave struck the *Santa Cruz*. She tottered, then heaved, and as if to avoid a greater blow, she seemed to leap out of the water.

Brien was thrown across the deck. He hit his head on a cask. A sailor, close by tried to grab the boy, as another giant wave rammed the ship and flung a mountain of water crashing over her decks.

In that moment, Brien was swept overboard.

The sailor made the sign of the cross. 'God be merciful to the lad,' was all he could say. There was nothing he could do.

The first light of day showed the destruction only too clearly.

Owen was grateful that he still had most of his cargo and all of his men. One of the masts was missing. That would further slow their progress. But it could be replaced when they landed in Spain.

He was told of Brien's death.

'Ach no! When did it happen?' Owen was visibly shaken. A man accustomed to battles and killings, yet when it came to this small boy, he had to turn his face aside for a moment.

Grainne was still below deck when her father told her. 'The wee lad,' was all she said, as if she were his mother. But in her mouth there was a sour taste.

It was not the first death at sea that she had known but Brien had a special place in her heart. She would always remember him.

A tear ran down her cheek then. Like her father, she tried to hide her grief.

'Perhaps it's better for Brien this way. He was such a small boy. I think he needed his mother and father. He had no one else in this world.' she said, trying to assuage her father's grief.

After that, Grainne took Brien's place for the rest of the voyage.

★

Blown off course by the storm, the ship took three days longer than it should.

At last the north-west coast of Spain was sighted.

Grainne, who knew from her classmates that Spain was a country of sunshine and warmth, couldn't wait to see this bright land and its people.

As the O'Malley ships drew close to the shore, Grainne thought they had somehow made a big mistake. Surely, they had been turned around in the storm?

This couldn't be Spain! Perhaps they were being fooled by the 'wee folk.' It had to be Ireland... silver mists, a rugged coastline, deep inlets, small fields, stone walls, grazing sheep and cattle, trees bent and huddled against the blasts of the Atlantic.

'Huh, so this is sunny Spain.' Grainne voiced her thoughts. 'Perhaps that's why my ancestors, the Milesians, came and took possession of Ireland. It looked so much like home to them.'

La Coruña was their first port of call.

As soon as they landed, Grainne asked her father to buy her some flowers.

Later when the sun was saying farewell to another day, Grainne said good-bye to Brien for the last time. Standing on a cliff high above the waters which had taken him so quickly and so cruelly, she flung the flowers as far as she could. Then turning her face to the heavens, she prayed: 'Jesu, good shepherd, please take your little lamb, Brien, to live with you. Amen.'

★

While the broken mast was being rebuilt, Owen contacted old friends. He bartered some goods, sold others, and bargained for wines and other native products.

Grainne insisted that he take on a large supply of citrus fruits. She knew he could sell them for twice what he paid for them.

It was a busy time.

Grainne learned much about the ways and customs of the Spanish people. She was proud of her command of the language. At times, she passed for a native lad with her dark eyes and sallow complexion.

The seaport city of Vigo was a bustling place when the *Santa Cruz* docked there a few days later.

Owen was disappointed, however, when he found that the prices of everything were much higher than the previous year. He was unable to buy all he wanted.

'Father,' said Grainne, who knew his thoughts. 'There are other ways of getting what you need.'

He looked at her. 'Are you suggesting that we take advantage of...?' he said, laughing. Her crafty scheming mind found a way out of all her problems.

'Who knows, Father, we might just happen to come across the right ship at the right time on our way home.' And she laughed with him.

They were two of a kind and that no one could deny.

The return journey was uneventful until they reached the south-west coast of Ireland.

Rounding the tip of Kerry near Dursey Island, the lookout called the alarm. 'Ship ahoy!'

There, sure enough, half hidden near the nibbled neck of land lay a caravel. The rays of the setting sun dancing on her brasses had betrayed her. 'Twas surely a Turkish pirates' vessel; one of those that had been plaguing the west coast for so many months.

Owen prayed that the same rays would not reveal his vessels to the enemy.

At once, he ordered the majority of his ships to change course. 'Due west, then north, and head for home.' He would allow his ship in the meantime to become a decoy for the enemy. By keeping the *Santa Cruz* close to the shoreline, he hoped to draw out the enemy while his other ships made their getaway.

Owen kept watch on the vessel for several hours. There was no change in her position.

'A crippled ship! It has to be!' Owen was thinking out loud. 'No reason otherwise to anchor in those waters.'

'*Dar Dia*! Father. 'Tis what we've been waiting for!' Grainne was impatient.

Owen looked at his daughter. She was scarcely more than a child. He hesitated... He didn't want to dismiss the idea out of hand.

She had experienced danger. She had not flinched in the face of death. Yet, did she really understand the risks involved in raiding a ship? Mayhap, a pirate ship?

'What's up, Father?' she asked.

'I'm thinking, it's one thing to raid an unsuspecting fishing boat but quite another to attack a Turkish pirate vessel,' he answered.

Grainne considered his words.

'You're right, of course. Still, she's probably a crippled vessel as you suspect...A pirate ship! The risk will be great, yes, but the spoils will be still greater.'

Again Owen studied his child. And again he asked himself, what kind of child had he sired.

He had never known her equal. Already, her thoughts out-stripped his own.

Her courage, daring, and willpower were the equal of grown men twice her age.

She was a compelling force. A rock of strength that even he, Owen 'Dubhdarra' O'Malley who was feared on land and sea, was unable to move. How often had he heard m'Lord Abbot say of her, 'Extraordinary... extraordinary!'

She had won the respect and loyalty of the men on his flagship. They admired her. She had not complained when things got tough. She had done her part, her share of the work, although, as yet, a child's share.

They could not accuse her of being a cry baby. Quite the contrary: she had helped with binding up wounds. And, after the storm, had even sewn a large gash in O'Reilly's shoulder where the falling mast had caught him.

A few, there were, who still held the old superstition that a female on board ship brought bad luck. And when the storm had done its worst and little Brien had lost his life, he heard them curse and swear and blame their plight on 'Granuaile.'

But Grainne had an answer for the ignorant, the unlettered of the crew. For when O'Toomey, the rope maker, with amulet in hand accused her, she was ready. And it made Owen proud of her again.

"Tis all your fault! You've brought the wrath of the sea *Bandia* upon us all. 'Tis unnatural...

'A woman on board ship
Will bring bad luck.
The words are older

Than the Holy Book.'

'You're a fool, Dermud O'Toomey,' retorted Grainne. 'Such crazy talk could cause more trouble than the storm. Cast off your pagan charm and ask your Christian God to forgive you.'

With such intelligence and common sense, Owen knew he didn't have to concern himself for his daughter's survival.

And now that better times and fairer weather had accompanied them on the return journey, these same men had changed their mind, and their moods. She, Grainne, it was, who had become their protector. He even heard old Toomey mutter in his beard, when he was within easy hearing of his Captain, 'If Grainne be with us, none shall do us harm.'

Owen thought a long time and his thoughts were deep, deep as the sea. He had a daughter the equal of none.

Then, as the sun sank into the depths of the western ocean, he made his decision.

The October moon was playing hide-and-seek with the clouds. A steady breeze was blowing from the south-west as the curragh moved quietly towards the shore.

Six men, led by Sean Mac Neil soon beached the boat and moved nimbly, stealthily over the rocks.

Their plan was to determine the identity of the ship, the nature of her cargo, the reason for its present position, and if possible the number of her crew.

As soon as they got close enough, Sean saw that the ship had run aground. A huge gash in her hull had indeed crippled the vessel. By the light of the moon, the name *Abdul Meijid* was visible. The O'Malley was right again.

The other men huddled on the rocks nearby. Sean rejoined them.

They waited and listened. Only the rapping of the breakers against the crippled ship, only the pounding of the waves in an nearby cave could be heard.

No sound came from within the ship. Where was the crew? They looked anxiously at one another.

In whispered tones, the men agreed that the crew had probably taken a small boat across to Dunsey Island in search of provisions. They may have been stranded in their present position for quite some time; run out of food, no doubt.

'God help the poor souls on Dunsey,' said one man as he crossed himself and continued to pray silently. 'Bloody murderin' savages,' he murmured.

Having come to this conclusion, Sean decided to board the ship. However, they must be careful; one man should remain to guard the curragh. Cormac was chosen, a young man who would surely get word back to the Captain if anything went awry.

Sean and his men broke into two groups. They would climb aboard at different places. With their knives between their teeth, they scampered up the sides and slipped on to the main deck of the caravel.

A small light was visible in the forecastle. Sean crept closer. He could see two men. Their turbaned heads bowed in concentration over their game of dice. The air was heavy with the pungent scent of opium.

Sean had seen enough. He slipped back into the shadows and soon joined his companions.

They, meantime, had checked the cargo. Satisfied that they had all the information needed by their Captain, they left the ship as quickly and silently as they had come.

The news caused quite a stir on the *Santa Cruz*. Italian wines, spices from the Orient, silks, brocades and porcelain, even gold pieces and precious jewels: there was a veritable treasure out there ready for the taking!

Grainne was so excited that she wanted to go immediately. Better to be caught by the returning pirates crowded into small boats unable to defend themselves, than to meet them head-on with guns blazing.

She was right.

The O'Malley set his course. He would pull in as close to the shore as possible. Then, the men would do their work with the smaller boats he kept lashed to the sides of his caravel.

The two Turkish guards were quickly dispatched. Within half an hour the *Abdul Meijid* was relieved of much of her wealth.

As O'Malley's men were returning with their last haul, the sound of foreign voices reached their ears.

They quickened their speed, and prayed the moon would cover her face. There had been enough killing for one night.

When they reached the *Santa Cruz* they were quickly hauled aboard.

And as the bulging sacks and heavy crates were being stacked, The O'Malley shouted and let the wind carry his words where they would.

'God bless Ireland, and the devil take her enemies!'

Owen had been lucky. The captured booty would make up for the loss he had suffered in Spain. For another year the O'Malleys and their followers would live well.

★

The homecoming was a joyous time for all except Grainne. She alone missed the wide open seas.

She loved to feel the churning waters beneath her feet. She liked to watch the rise and fall of the constant rhythm of the waves. Her heart sang to the music of the breakers. Her life's breath she inhaled from the breath of the sea. She tasted its taste in the kelp that she constantly rolled between her teeth.

The sea was her friend, her teacher, and, apart from her father, her only love.

'The sea's in your blood.' How often had she heard her father tell her? From the time she could barely toddle, she knew what he meant and agreed with him.

The sea fed her mind and heart as surely as it gave nourishment to her body.

Grainne could not imagine life without the sea and as a consequence she was never really happy when she was forced to give it up for even a short while.

The feasting and the merrymaking lasted well into the morning hours.

The tables in the dining-hall were lavishly stocked. Large wooden platters of hot meats: mutton, venison, and beef, as well as heaped bowls of vegetables were placed at convenient distances. Tankards of ale, jugs of mead, flagons of wine, and mugs of buttermilk were also within easy reach. Small loaves of barley bread and larger rye cakes were stacked on both ends of the low tables.

Cu and Boru and the other hounds waited patiently for the bones. Their intelligent eyes watching everything; they were intent, eager to obey the master's slightest wish.

O'Rourke took his place near the fire. He ate and warmed his old bones and prepared for an evening of entertaining.

Grainne sat between her father and mother at dinner. Her hair had an extra couple of inches to its length so her mother was comforted that she would soon look halfway normal and not a wild uncouth creature.

'Now that you have had your wish, Grainne, and have been to Spain, I hope you'll settle down and think of your future,' she remarked.

Grainne didn't know what her mother meant. Surely she didn't think that one trip to Spain was going to teach her all she would have to know? How did she expect her to learn her father's trade, his contacts, his tricks, if she didn't accompany him on all his trips?

At that moment, she was tired. The rich food, the warmth, all made her sleepy. She would not even try to answer her mother's question.

Her father came to her aid. ''Tis been a long hard day,' he said, and he was about to tell her mother of their narrow escape off the Kerry coast but thought better of it. What she didn't know wouldn't trouble her, he decided.

So the cycle of events continued and Grainne gained years and experience and knowledge while, at the same time, she gained physical strength and growth.

Chapter Thirteen

Grainne celebrated her fourteenth birthday. She was now at an age when most girls were thinking of marriage.

She had reached her full height of five feet seven. And thoroughbred that she was, she was lean, long-legged and shapely.

Grainne was not considered beautiful. Some called her handsome. Her dark brown eyes were alert, warm, and intelligent. She had a straight nose, a strong jaw, and full shapely lips. Her unique husky laugh revealed strong, white, even teeth. Only her glossy black hair was truly beautiful. But Grainne, being who she was, paid no attention to it. It floated about her, driven by wind and rain, and her own excess of energy, like so much seaweed on the turbulent sea waters.

'I'll not wear that outlandish gown. I'll not be tied up like a stuffed goose. Nor will I parade about like a popinjay,' she declared. Grainne threw the new gown, made by her mother, across the floor.

Cait, the serving maid, put her hands to her mouth in horror. 'Oh, m'Lady Grainne! I... I... think...'

'Cait, you're not here to think. Give me my plain, black, silk *leine*. And take that ridiculous thing they call a farthingale out and burn it.'

Grainne was furious. She was expected to attend a banquet to honor her father and mother, a lavish affair prepared by The O'Flaherty to which they had been invited. But Grainne also knew that behind the outward appearances, the real reason for the celebration was Grainne herself.

During the winter months, her mother had finally convinced her father that something had to be done about his grown-up daughter.

How often had she overheard her mother's words. 'Right connections. A suitable husband. She should be thinking of marriage, not romping about with common sailors on her father's ships.'

In the end, Owen had spoken to Grainne. 'What's a man to do? I had to promise that I'd at least try to find the right man,' he told her.

'Oh, Father, I don't want to get married... well not yet. I need to be free a little longer.'

But when Owen O'Malley did give the matter some consideration, he was at a loss as to where he might find this suitable husband.

He spoke to Margaret. 'The only eligible bachelor is young Donal O'Flaherty.' In mentioning Donal, Owen had hoped to keep his daughter by his side for many years yet to come.

The O'Flaherty had just submitted to the English King Henry. No daughter of his could possibly marry a traitor. He hadn't counted on Margaret's reaction.

Her beautiful blue eyes lit up at the mention of the O'Flaherty name.

'Now you don't mean to tell me you want our Grainne to marry a jellyfish?' said Owen.

'A jellyfish! What do you mean?' replied his wife.

'Margaret, you know very well that The O'Flaherty has bowed the knee to the English King.'

'Oh, Owen, you can't be serious. It's only lip service. Times are changing. One has to compromise.'

'Compromise! Surely you're not saying...!'

Owen was hurt. His own wife! It wasn't possible. An O'Malley submit to the *Sasanach* after more than a thousand years of ruling their own lands in their own way?

'No, I'll not do it. I'd rather see her shut up in a convent than submit to that insult!' he thundered.

To settle the matter, Grainne herself persuaded her father that an O'Flaherty would be the best choice – if a husband had to be considered at that time. She would take care of the 'small matter' of submission to the *Sasanach* later.

With the O'Flaherty lands directly to the south and adjoining their own, one day, she reasoned, she would rule almost the whole of Connaght. She would be Queen of Connaght, and no English monarch would dare regard her as anything less.

Grainne didn't care what happened anywhere else. Her father's lands and the seas around them were her only concern. If, by marrying Donal O'Flaherty and thus uniting these two powerful families, she could make the region stronger, she was willing to do so.

Word was sent to The O'Flaherty. And, in due course, word came back: the O'Malley and his family would be welcomed in Bunowen Castle.

Grainne waited for her parents to accompany her to the large dining hall. She had decided, in the end, to wear the new gown but without the fashionable farthingale. As a result, the skirt was far too long. To prevent herself from tripping over it, she had prevailed upon Cait to stitch a large hem on it. When the job was done, Grainne pulled it on.

It stood out at the end like a bell. Cait wasn't sure. She had never seen the likes of it anywhere before.

'Twill do fine. We'll call it the "red bell,"' said Grainne. 'Maybe I'll start a fashion of my own, like Elizabeth of England.'

She laughed at her image in the bronze mirror. 'Why not? You're far better than she. Can she boast of a family whose blood was royal as far back as the fourth century? Surely not.' She addressed her image, and her serving maid, Cait, thought she was losing her mind.

As she awaited her parents in the passageway outside their bedroom, her only concern was that her father might forget to insist that the wedding ceremony be performed in both traditions: according to the Brehon Laws and the Catholic Church.

Margaret stepped into the hallway. Dressed in cool shades of blue and lavender silk, she wore a delicate lace outer garment. From head to toe, she looked every inch the Royal Princess that she was. A beautiful diadem of rubies and a dainty ruby neckband enhanced her natural beauty.

These jewels had been a special gift from Owen for their twentieth wedding anniversary. He had purchased them in Bordeaux on his last trip abroad.

Owen was deeply in love with his beautiful wife. Grainne saw how he looked at her. She knew how proud he was to accompany her on such an occasion, for Margaret was known to be the most beautiful woman in all of Connaght.

But if Margaret was beautiful, surely her father, Owen, had to be the most handsome man in all Ireland. He certainly was at that moment.

An Irish gentleman of the highest order, he was dressed as befitted his rank and the occasion.

His tall lean body was in perfect health. He had strength and vitality. Clad in black velvet trews and silk ivory *leine*, the wide sleeves of which were colorfully embroidered, he also wore a new leather jerkin. A sash woven of golden threads carried a bejeweled skene at his right side, for he was a prince and had the right to do so. Lesser men might leave their weapons without when attending such a gathering, but The O'Malley was no mean man.

He flipped his chieftain's cloak aside. As he did so, Grainne admired the Tara brooch that held it in place: a sparkling gold piece studded with emeralds.

For a moment neither of them saw Grainne. They were wrapped up in each other. Owen kissed his wife and as they turned to descend the stone stairs to join the host, Margaret gasped.

It took a moment for her to find her tongue. 'What on earth have you done with your gown?' she asked.

'I'll not be bound in a cage,' she answered. 'It was a most ridiculous contraption.'

It was too late to do anything.

Margaret was forced to endure yet another humiliation.

Owen, seeing his pretty wife so downcast, tried to cheer her. 'At least, be thankful she hasn't appeared in her trews,' he whispered.

As Grainne walked behind her parents into the great hall of Bunowen Castle, she didn't care what anyone thought about her.

She knew what she wanted. She knew where she was going. She knew who she was.

The festivities began with a blessing by the local bishop. Then a round of toasts.

'*Sláinte mait aguib*,'[1] said The O'Flaherty, holding up his glass.

'*Sláinte's beannact*,'[2] answered Owen, The O'Malley.

The banquet that followed left no doubt about O'Flaherty's hospitality and when it was finished, it was O'Malley's duty to thank his host with a speech and to praise his glorious name.

Concluding, Owen stressed the importance, especially in the changing and troubled times through which they were going, that the great and proud Irish families be united. 'We are all Gaels. Our roots are deep in this gentle land. Our heritage is second to none. It is a heritage of beauty in art, poetry, literature, and music. Let's not lose it.

'A heritage devoted to ideals rather than material gain. A heritage of vitality and the will to survive, as well as courage in battle.

---

[1] *Sláinte mait aguib* – good health to you.
[2] *Sláinte's beannact* – health and blessing.

'Let me say, my friends, that we Gaels should cherish that which has been handed down to us, and let our motto always be the words of the *Caoilte* to St. Patrick, "Truth in our hearts, and strength in our arms and fulfillment in our tongues."'

The applause was loud and long. And Owen knew that he had stirred the heart of the great O'Flaherty.

And Grainne knew, that in time, the words of old Maeve would be fulfilled.

Chapter Fourteen

Grainne sat on her favorite rock looking out to sea.

How often, as a child, had she sat in this very same place, waiting...'

Waiting for her beloved father.

Waiting and watching. Watching and waiting for the first stirrings way out on the far off horizon.

The anticipation, the excitement as the specks took form – a sail, a hull, and then, as if by magic, a flotilla!

Galleys, caravels, carracks, longboats, and for company, the curraghs and fishing boats that had joined them at the mouth of the Bay. Sails fat against the wind rising and falling on welcoming waves.

She looked at the incoming tide. Happy waters. Clear, crystal, sparkling now with a myriad gems.

The sea had always been her friend. She did not doubt that it would continue to be a lifelong friend.

How well she knew it. Its moods: dark, sullen, foreboding, moments of sinister thoughts, an outburst, then days of tempestuous fury. Or tranquil, happy hours – laughing, playful times, when sunny faced white caps kissed, and danced and chased each other to the shore.

Yes, Grainne knew the sea.

Cradled in its waters from birth, she heard its lullabies as they lulled her to sleep. She knew its voice and the sound of its cries before she heard her own. She tasted its salty lips and felt its soothing silky embrace when summer suns were not too kind. And every day and at all times, she smelled its tangy breath.

And Grainne felt secure. For the sea would always be there. As long as the world lasted, the sea would wrap it around, protecting it.

She stood up. It was growing dark. The tide had turned. He wouldn't come today.

Grainne was now promised in marriage to Donal O'Flaherty, nicknamed '*Donal-an-Chogaidh!*' (Donal of The Battles).

As the oldest son of Gilleduff O'Flaherty, the castles at Bunowen and Ballinahinch were his. He was also recognized, according to Irish custom, as the tanist. He it was that would inherit the lands and would be head of the clan. He, it was who would rule over Iar Connacht.

Grainne thought of her future. Her upcoming marriage. Her husband-to-be.

It was for him she had been waiting.

Was it a sign? Had he forgotten? Too busy fighting? Another battle? Surely a waste of time and property. Futile...! His talents and strength would be better served were he to use them against those who would rob him of his country.

'Well,' Grainne declared, 'I'll not wait for him again.'

★

Ever since the family's visit to Bunowen Castle, Margaret's attitude to Grainne had changed. She smiled at her more often. She even tried to compliment her, that is whenever she could find something about which she could compliment her.

Perhaps, she thought, as a mother she had been too critical. There must be something about her daughter if the O'Flaherty was eager to accept her into the clan.

So Margaret puzzled over the questions that were uppermost in her mind while she prepared her daughter's trousseau.

She would see to it that the girl had what was expected of a young woman of her station: fine gowns and shoes and cloaks and furs for her wardrobe. She might never wear any of them, but she wouldn't leave her father's house without the best.

And then, there was the household goods: blankets, sheets, and down quilts, an assortment of tableware; bowls, platters, cruets, decanters, mugs, and jugs. The lists seemed endless. But it was expected and Margaret would fulfill all her responsibilities. 'Never let it be said that an O'Malley didn't have the best,' she was heard to say.

The wedding would take place in the spring of her sixteenth year. In this matter, she didn't have much say. The parents on both sides had the responsibility of taking care of all that had to do with the marriage ceremonies.

Grainne really didn't care, however. She would put up with the inconvenience of wearing a wedding dress, of being gawked at for several hours and the tiresome formalities that went along with such functions.

'I'll have the last laugh,' she said. For when they'd had their say, the criticizers and the jealous as well as the few well-wishers, she would be the winner in the end.

She would be Queen of Connaght!

But that time was seven or eight months away. In the meantime there was another trip to Spain. Donal-an-Chogaidh might come calling if he wished; she wouldn't be there.

One more trip! Once more on the high seas with her beloved father.

'Oh, Father, why wasn't I born a boy?'

Grainne's heart spoke rather than her lips. 'Had I been a boy I could have sailed with you for the rest of your life.'

For a moment she was downcast. She just couldn't imagine life without her father. The years had gone by too fast.

Then her practical nature took control. She wouldn't be that far away. It would be easy enough to visit him from time to time. She might even slip away and join him on a trip or two to the Continent.

She convinced herself that indeed she'd have to visit him. He needed her advice. He had come to depend on her. He was growing older. And if that wasn't enough, there was always the responsibility that she knew the future held for her: the command of her father's ships, the leadership of his followers, the rule over his lands and vast holdings.

She had made up her mind that on this next trip she would Captain the ship. She would take her father's flagship the *Santa Cruz* into her own hands. And,

while he was still there to guide her, she would sail it
to Spain. She would be the one to barter, and haggle
and sell. She would be the one to buy and bargain and
finally to sail home again proud as she stood in the
forecastle of a proud ship.

Grainne, Sailor Princess, would become Queen of
The Seas!

★

Grainne Ni Malley had never bowed her head to any
man. Now that she was betrothed to an O'Flaherty, it
was whispered, she would have to watch her step.

Donal O'Flaherty's family was great and powerful.
A very large family. The Chieftain, whose place Donal
would one day take, had many duties and responsibilities. Like the kings of other lands, The O'Flaherty had
his fortresses and castles where members of noble but
lesser families paid him homage and served him in
professions passed on from father to son.

The O'Canavans were his physicians; the
O'Colgans his standard-bearers, and the O'Maelampaills his *brehons*.

> *The names are old*
> *And the list is long.*
> *For many noble houses*
> *Have come and gone.*
> *Yet, The O'Flaherty family*
> *Lives, and it will live on.*
> *So sang the bard and his words were true.*

Donal was a fiery youth. Some called him handsome, and perhaps they were right. He had a head of brown wavy hair, blue eyes set wide apart, a strong straight nose, and a firm mouth. His complexion contrasted with that of Grainne's, for his skin was fair, and the winds and rains and the summer suns had given it a ruddy glow.

He was a tall man with strong limbs. His muscles were well-developed, for Donal was a fighting man and spent much of his time playing at war or making war.

His reaction to the choice of bride they had made for him was favorable at the time. She was a woman of good breeding, well formed and in excellent health.

He was first and foremost a fighting man. A girl like Grainne would not flinch at the sight of a soldier's wounds, nor would she fret when he was obliged to be away from home.

For Donal had no intention of changing his ways after the marriage.

Chapter Fifteen

It was a glorious morning in early July, fifteen forty-six. The bells at the Murrisk Abbey rang out the news.

Grainne Ni Malley.

Donal O'Flaherty.

Outside the Castle and leading to the Abbey the pennants of the O'Malley and O'Flaherty families flapped in the sweet-scented breezes.

Inside the church, built by her great-grandparents in 1457 for the Augustinian Friars, the banners of the Gaelic lords from many parts of Ireland were displayed. The O'Donnell, the O'Sullivan Bearra, the O'Neill, the O'Hara, O'Connor, O'Kelly, O'Dowd: too many to count were their number on that day.

The nuns from the nearby convent sang the hymns and chants. Their voices pure as the angels whose images they so often contemplated. The convent had also been built by Grainne's ancestor, The Lady Maeve Ni Conchobhar, wife of Lord Dermot O'Malley.

The wedding procession was forming outside the church. The Lord Abbot, now bent with years, but still determined to be present at the wedding of The O'Malley's daughter, tottered in his gold vestments. He was followed by a long line of monks in flowing white robes.

The Lord Abbot was growing a little impatient. Without Grainne he couldn't proceed. What was the girl doing? Where was she? He still thought of her as a child.

He had hoped she would be reasonable on this her wedding day.

During the past few weeks she had caused him many sleepless nights. Her demands were most unusual. Who else but Grainne would refuse to be married in the true faith unless she could also be wed according to the Brehon Laws? In the end, he was forced, for the sake of her immortal soul, to allow the service to be performed. But he did make one provision. The Catholic Matrimonial Rites must take place first.

'Has Grainne come yet?' asked the Abbot, and turned to his assistant, Friar Fergus. Little beads of perspiration had appeared on his forehead. His miter tilted to one side. It's an extraordinary hot day, thought the Abbot.

'No, m'Lord, I don't see her.'

And while the Abbot waited, Grainne grew impatient with the maid who was doing her hair.

The Lady Margaret had insisted that the long thick mane be plaited in several different coils. The result would have been very elegant had not Grainne considered it an unnecessary torture. The combs and pins needed to keep these coils in place were sticking into her head and causing her such unaccustomed irritation that she decided she had had enough. At the last moment, she undid the lot and let her hair fall in its natural way.

When her mother saw what she had done she almost lost her composure.

But there were so many lords and ladies standing around, she bit her tongue instead. She tried to smile, but it turned into a grimace in spite of herself.

Finally, a compromise was reached. Grainne allowed her maid to gather her hair on both sides into two gold lock-rings. She had no intention of wearing the usual rolled linen head cloth.

The gown was brought. It had been stored for several weeks in one of Lady Margaret's oak chests. A magnificent silk gown. Her father had sent to Italy for the exquisite material.

Tiny pearls adorned the neck and the full sleeves were finished at the wrists in similar fashion. A mantle displaying the O'Malley Coat of Arms with its proud emblems of power on land and seas was placed over her shoulders. Ten young ladies-in-waiting, chosen from the great Gaelic families, held the mantle so that all could see and admire. The magnificent embroidery, so painstakingly executed by the nuns at the Murrisk Convent, was a work of art. The rare gems, worked into the family's motto: *Terra-Marique-Potens*, sparked in the changing lights.

Before Grainne left the Castle, there was one more thing she stopped to do.

Cu, her faithful wolfhound was sitting quietly close by. She called him and bending whispered in his ear. The great dog's intelligent bright eyes lit up. They both looked at each other a moment. It seemed, to those looking on, that Cu smiled.

'Cu,' a lady-in-waiting repeated. 'Doesn't the hound have any name? "Hound" seems odd.'

Grainne turned. 'Why should it be odd?' she replied. 'This is the greatest wolfhound in all Ireland. He is *An Cu* (the Hound). He needs no other name.'

At last Grainne was ready.

Down the Castle steps and into the noonday sunshine they slowly wound their way, ladies-in-waiting, attendants, flower-girls and pageboys, and, finally, Grainne and her train-bearers.

The cheering was deafening. Some cast flower petals, others waved reeds or leafy branches. The old ones prayed for long life and happiness and many children. The young laughed and joked and thought of their own marriages.

They had come from the far reaches of The O'Malley and O'Flaherty territories.

From the islands, the mountains, and the flat lands. They had come from the north and the south, great lords and ladies, from mighty castles, and lowly folk from small one-roomed cabins. All wished to show their love or loyalty, or both.

The Bay was a floating town. Boats of every size and shape, banners streaming, flags flying. Such a sight was seen once in a lifetime.

The Abbot could no longer take the hot sun. A stool was brought for him.

'I confirmed this young woman some ten or eleven years ago. Even then she kept everyone waiting,' said the Abbot.

'What did she do, M'Lord?' asked The O'Donnell, who overheard the remark.

'She hid and couldn't be found for hours. When, at last, she was discovered, she started a terrible hullabaloo. I heard her myself. "I'm not going in... I'm not going in there... That old man will not slap me."' The Abbot chuckled.

'Grainne's not one to be pushed around. A mind of her own, eh?' The O'Donnell spoke.

Owen 'Dubhdarra' O'Malley waited for his daughter outside the great entrance doors of the church. He saw her coming and went to meet her. She took and held his hand a moment, but could not look at him.

The procession started up again. The nuns repeated the entrance psalm. The noble lords and ladies waiting inside made room for the Abbot and the monks. With candles and bells, and led by a young acolyte carrying a crucifix, they slowly made their way toward the main altar.

The crowd inside caught sight of Grainne. Then came a craning of necks and a forward movement.

Grainne hesitated before starting into the dark interior of the church. She looked toward the sea.

It was a calm, a tranquil sea. And Grainne, ever attuned to its mood, had a quiet but sad heart.

Her childhood was over. When she re-emerged into the sunlight, she thought, she would be a married woman. Her life changed forever.

And so on this her wedding day, Grainne's heart was heavy.

'Grainne, my Sailor Princess.' Her father's voice reminded her that she had delayed too long.

She looked at him. They saw only each other. She saw the moisture cloud the smile he tried to give her.

He saw the tear that fell from her long dark lashes.

They had no need of words. Their hearts and souls were one.

Lord Owen 'Dubhdarra' O'Malley held his head high. And as Grainne took his arm, she did the same.

They walked slowly and deliberately into the church, past the gawking crowds and the mumbled approval.

At the altar, Donal stepped forward. But before Owen let go of her hand, he suddenly, impulsively took her in his arms and kissing her cheek, he whispered, 'Remember, I'll always be with you, my Grainne.'

Before she turned to ascend the altar steps, she saw him. Cu, her faithful friend, was walking quietly but in his own proud way up the center aisle. When their eyes met, Grainne saw Cu smile. She patted his noble head before he sat, himself, down at the left side of the altar.

Grainne also saw how the Abbot opened his mouth to object, then quickly raising his hand pretended to yawn.

'This is Grainne,' he mumbled. 'One has to expect the unexpected.'

The ceremony was long and elaborate. The Abbot too old and too tired to support the endless litanies, prayers, and blessings retired to his rooms before the conclusion.

Back at the Castle, under an arbor decorated with wild flowers and sea shells, the *Brehon*, O'Maelampaills, patiently waited. He sat on a rock, his dark flowing robes spread out and falling to the ground. In his hand a copy of the *Senchus Mor*. His knowledge of the laws was such that he had no need of the book. But, in the presence of such an august gathering, he wished to look and act the part of the great judge that he was.

After some introductory words, the *Brehon* turned to the section entitled 'Bargains, Contracts, and Engagements between man and man.'

It was Grainne's wish that her new husband be reminded of the ancient Gaelic laws of marriage. The *Brehon* had been told to emphasize the passage 'marriage for a year certain.' This law allowed divorce after one year if the couple were not suited to each other.

Grainne wasn't sure which law she would follow: the law of the Church or the Brehon, but in her mind she had taken every precaution. Like a true sea captain, she would be prepared for turbulent waters and rough seas.

'Any port in a storm.' She knew the saying well.

★

The festivities lasted a week. By the time they were over and Grainne and Donal had said farewell to all their guests, they were ready to depart for Bunowen Castle.

As the ship pulled out from the shore, Grainne's heart was full to overflowing with pain.

Her father had not come to see her off. He refused to say good-bye.

'Sure you'll be back again soon, girl. 'Tis only a few miles down the coast you'll be. I'll be banging on your door in a week or two.' He tried to cover up his own pain in a flood of words.

'I know... I know,' was all she could answer.

The sun had past its zenith. They could not tarry too long in the Bay even though Grainne wanted to linger.

She watched the islands that she knew so well slip by. A mist blurred her view. But the sky and all around was crystal clear. Close by the shallows where she learned to swim were only little pools now, their size diminished by her increasing years.

She lifted her eyes to the Castle, its granite exterior was a jewel of many colors in the afternoon sunlight.

Her beloved home was growing smaller as the distance grew. Soon she would be unable to see it at all.

Grainne choked back a sob.

Donal was beside her. He mustn't know.

They rounded the headland, the outcropping of jagged black rocks where as a little girl she waited... waited for him to come home.

Then she saw him!

Gallant, handsome, head held high. Her beloved father had taken her place!

His saffron *leine* was a stark contrast to the gray and black rocks. He waved an ivory handkerchief and waited... waited till the ship was a mere speck on the golden horizon.

Bibliography

Fairburn, Eleanor, *The White Seahorse*, Dublin, Wolfhound Press, 1985

Chambers, Anne, *Granuaile*, Dublin, Wolfhound Press 1983

Kilroy, Patricia, *The Story of Connemara*, Dublin, Gill and Macmillan, 1989

Rafterey, Joseph, *The Celts*, Dublin, Mercier Press, 1964

Mac Manus, Seamus, *The Story Of The Irish Race*, Connecticut, Devin-Adair Co., 1979

Llywelyn, Morgan, *Grainne*, New York, Crown Publishing, 1986

Chamberlin, E.R., *Everyday Life in Renaissance Times*, London, Carousel Book, 1965

Llywelyn, Morgan, *Bard*, Boston, Houghton Mifflin Company, 1984

Herity, Michael, *Gold in Ancient Ireland*, Irish Environmental Library Series, No. 15

McKendrick, Melveena, *Spain*, New York, American Heritage Publishing Co., 1972

Rook, David, *Run Wild, Run Free*, New York, Scholastic Services, 1967